Sorrowmouth

First published in Great Britain in 2022 by Black Shuck Books

Cover design by WHITEspace
from "The Ghost of a Flea"
by William Blake
Courtesy of the Tate Gallery

Set in Caslon by WHITEspace
www.white-space.uk

978-1-913038-74-8

Sorrowmouth

by
Simon Avery

BLACK
SHUCK
BOOKS

One

Underhill tried to keep walking, but it was a futile gesture. Momentum would not carry him beyond this sickness. From one roadside memorial to the next; miles of trudging around Hastings since six a.m. After twelve hours he arrived at the seafront and his final destination of the day. The heat had been almost intolerable.

A council van was parked beside the promenade. A man was crouched at the railings where the memorial had been arranged for the past month. Beyond him the sea was a calm blue mirror, the sun still high and undimmed. Underhill's shirt was soaked to his back. He paused at the traffic lights, the bright lights and tinny music of the arcades chattering at his ears like mosquitos. He disliked the gaudy confusion of the seafront; the handful of tourists and the stinking cafes and the pier. Hastings had been in steady decline for years. Sometimes Underhill imagined the sea rushing in over the shingles and the promenade, across the busy road and through the town, claiming everything for itself. There was nothing worth saving. The world he'd once glimpsed as a child was long gone. It was the ghost of a memory to him now.

Underhill's rucksack was already heavy with items he had stolen from other memorials: a painted stone from Chowns Hill; a rusting watch outside the Spar on The Ridge; a faded photograph just down from the Co-op on Bohemia Road. These objects were loaded with significance and left at the roadside by grieving families in the forlorn conviction that a revenant lingered there, wondering if they'd been missed or abandoned to the in-between. A split-second of a driver's attention wandering, a child running out into the road; lives subsequently upturned, sometimes wholly unrecoverable from what they had been just a moment before. These shrines were replete with the reverberations from that event; Underhill sometimes imagined he could feel all that grief, all that sorrow, suspended in the air around these memorials; an echo of screeching brakes and squealing tires, the briefest cry of shock or pain, the all-encompassing silence that ensued. The silence of sorrow.

"You family, mate?"

Underhill hadn't realised that he'd gotten so close to the council worker. The question lifted him abruptly out of the reverie that the day had swaddled him in. The man had a soft, doughy face and short, stubby fingers. The fluorescent jacket swamped him.

"No," Underhill said, without thinking, "friend of the family." He glanced down at the memorial. There were some cheap supermarket carnations withered in cellophane, droplets of rain beading in the wells of the petals. A damp teddy bear and the ubiquitous 'ghost' bicycle, painted white and tied to the railings beside the road. The victim's name, everywhere: *Dearest Daniel. Beloved Daniel. I miss you, Daniel.*

"I know Daniel's mum."

The council worker sat back on his heels. "Right. Council has implemented a by-law for these roadside memorials – thirty days and we have to come and dismantle them. I don't agree with it, to be honest, and I suppose if it wasn't high summer, they wouldn't be so strict about it, but the tourists don't want to see this kind of thing, do they? Not when they're on holiday."

"No, I suppose not," Underhill said.

"The mother going to want any of this back, do you think?"

Underhill shrugged.

"Do me a favour and have a look? See that she gets it back. I need to get this stuff cleared before I clock off."

Nestled deep within the folds of the cards and flowers Underhill found a strip of photo booth pictures. A young man, his face flushed, his hair cropped close to his skull, and a girl with a bright smile, planting a kiss on his cheek. In the second photo she was glancing uncertainly beyond the curtain and then in the third, her arms were flung around the boy. Faces that suggested that life was long and brilliant and love had infused every atom of their body. Underhill slipped the photo strip, the mouldy teddy bear and all of the cards into his rucksack for later and stepped aside.

"Fucking joyriders. Lad was on his bike. That's what I heard." The council worker started lifting the things away from the railing and into a black sack. A couple of minutes and it was all gone, the memory of it removed.

"Yeah, I think so. They hit Daniel and didn't stop." Underhill didn't know if this was true, but it seemed likely.

The council worker nodded as he snipped the clips that held the white bicycle to the rail. He lifted it into the back of his van. He was done here. Already thinking about getting back home, dinner on the table, TV, playing with the kids. "You see the lady gets those things, all right?" he said as he slammed the door to his van.

Underhill nodded. He stood at the roadside where the memorial had been, unwilling to look away from that place in case he too forgot what it represented to someone. Sorrowmouth stood beside him, scraping his thorn against his bowl to express his displeasure. Tomorrow it would be the anniversary of his mother's death, and this was what Sorrowmouth had reduced him to. Every year, it got a little bit worse.

"Yes," Underhill said under his breath. "Yes, *I know.*"

Two

The boy's mother arrived later on, just as the sun was starting to sink on the horizon. Underhill was still there, sitting on the promenade wall, finishing off a bag of chips. He'd washed down his medication with a can of Coke. The woman was drunk, that much was quite apparent. He noticed her making her uncertain way along the seafront, pausing only to take long eager swigs from her can of lager, as if it was the only thing to sustain her on her trek here. Underhill didn't speak for a moment; he waited for her to walk past the place where the memorial had been, then pause, realising that she'd strayed too far. She glanced back in indecision. Her fist closed around the almost empty can. She had skin like leather, hard features, heavily applied make-up, long, bleached hair. She had a beautiful silk scarf around her throat, otherwise her clothes were plain: leggings, a t-shirt, a loose cardigan, some worn ballet-flats. She was wreathed in soft spirals of silver and black and red, the colours of her grief. She glanced at Underhill then at the place on the railings where the memorial had been. Underhill could see her bewilderment turning quickly to indignation.

"They took it," he said finally. "Your memorial."

"Who?" Her eyes were glassy, but there was a clear note of fury in her voice.

"The council," he said. "New by-laws." Underhill explained what the council worker had told him.

"They took," she said, "everything?"

"There's this—" Underhill reached into his holdall and took out the strip of photos and the teddy bear. He handed them to the woman.

She stared at them for a moment, tears instantly spilling down her stiff cheeks. Her fingernails were long and professionally painted. She could barely hold the photo-strip. "They had no right to do this," she said finally. "It's only been a month since, since…" She trailed away, glancing behind her at the cars passing on the busy road. All the sad little details of the town were fading behind the lights illuminating the strip. Underhill could hear some of the homeless population of Hastings congregating on the lower deck of the promenade, zombied on Spice and cheap cans of Carbon White. The heat had diminished and there was a welcome breeze now. Underhill's shirt was dry again but the exertions of the day hung heavily on his limbs.

"I kept all the things I thought you might want," Underhill offered, getting to his feet. He rooted in his holdall for the cards and handed them to her. "They were just going to chuck them away," he said. "It seemed like a waste."

She looked at Underhill properly this time, finally seeing him, appraising him. She touched her pretty bright scarf, her hair. "Why?" she asked.

He shrugged.

"It's nice of you." She took a final swig of the lager and walked away to drop it into a bin.

Sorrowmouth stepped forward with his thorn and Underhill said firmly but underneath his breath: "No. Not yet."

He heard Sorrowmouth hiss through his teeth but remain where he was.

"I liked what you wrote," Underhill offered when the woman returned. "In the cards to Daniel, I mean." He put a hand to his face. "I hope you don't mind my looking at the messages."

Her gaze was unfocused again. She was closer now. He could smell the booze on her breath; beer and the harder stuff.

"What I wrote?" she said.

"About the angels surrounding him, lifting him up towards heaven."

Her smile was stiff and fresh tears dripped from her eyes onto her hands.

"'Angels all around you all the days of your life,'" he said, quoting verbatim, the message she had written on the card to her dead son. "I hope you don't mind," he repeated.

She shook her head. She swayed beneath the streetlight and he reached out a hand to steady her. She took hold of his arm and blinked, once, twice. "My name," she began and then hesitated as if she didn't remember. "It's Mary," she said. And then, "Would you like to come back to the house? For a drink, I mean?"

Underhill gave the impression that he was giving the question some thought. He could feel Sorrowmouth at his shoulder, his fingers curling around his thorn, hypnotised by the bright swirls of anguish in the air. Scaly skin blushing in the moonlight. Heat rolling off him.

Underhill followed Mary along the promenade and up the Old London Road as the last of the light fled behind them. Mary led them through a warren of little streets until they reached Mount Pleasant Road. They stopped frequently here as Mary appeared to know almost every one of the streets' occupants, and felt obliged to engage in five minutes of idle gossip. At an off-license Underhill paid for a twelve-pack of Carling and a three litre bottle of White Lighting. Mary bought cigarettes. She knew the quiet middle-aged Indian man who served her from behind a glass screen; her voice was too loud in the cramped shop. Underhill stood, uncomfortable in the bright light while Mary focused on counting out coins and placing them into the drawer.

She lived not far away in a third floor council flat. Kids shuffling around them as Underhill and Mary made their way up the staircase to the flat – lippy little shits with shaved heads and shiny phones.

Mary's flat was little more than four narrow rooms and a balcony, choked with a profusion of plants that flowed over rails spattered with pigeon-shit. It was clean but the smell of years of cigarette smoke had bled into the fibres of every surface. The wallpaper and the blinds were turning yellow at the edges, just like Mary's fingers. Underhill stood awkwardly in the little living room, staring at the mantlepiece which was crowded with framed photographs of her dead son. Sorrowmouth skulked in the shadowy hallway, his shoulders bunched against the ceiling, a pinched look on his face.

Mary opened the new box of cigarettes and poured the White Lightning into pint glasses for herself and Underhill. They sat on the small sofa together. She tossed the cushions to the floor and delicately moved her hair out of her face.

Mary went through the cards from the memorial and read each one in turn. "This one is from Daniel's girlfriend," she said. It read: *I miss you. I will always love you. I will never forget you as long as I live. Love Mandy.*

"Last I heard she'd moved in with a bloke down the street who won twenty grand on the scratch cards," Mary said. Underhill didn't detect even a flicker of irritation at Mandy's apparent capriciousness.

"What happened?" Underhill asked. "To your boy?"

Mary took a long drag on her cigarette. She sat forward with her elbows on her knees as if to brace herself. "Daniel was killed," she said, with a far-off look on her face, "by a joy rider. They cruise up and down that strip all night, they do, racing each other. It's like a sport to them." She paused, her voice brittle with emotion. "You know what lads are like these days. Nothing else better to do with their time. Goading the police, robbing people." Mary exhaled a plume of smoke and glanced out at the bright flowers on her balcony. "The terrible fucking thing is I know half of them, *and* their parents. I see them every bastard day and I can't prove which of them it was, but they *know*, they do, and they just walk right past me, and I want to fucking *scream* at them, at all of them."

Underhill saw Sorrowmouth stooped in the doorway with his bowl and thorn, mottled skin burnished gold in the lamp glow, beady eyes beseeching him. Underhill nodded and he dipped his head under the doorframe and into the room, towering over both Underhill and Mary. Mary continued, her words beginning to slur.

"I think, no, *I know* that if I didn't have my beliefs, you know my absolute belief in, well, in angels, guardian angels, all around us, around me, well, I wouldn't have gotten through these last few weeks."

She glanced up, beyond where Sorrowmouth's face hung like a stiff mask in the cloud of cigarette smoke and saw something else entirely. She closed her eyes and smiled an entirely benign smile at the very notion of her personal angels. There were some crude and disappointingly prosaic paintings on the wall around the fire of them floating in the air, their wings outstretched, lit up with a golden glow that Underhill remembered like the tattered fragments of an ancient dream. Angels looking over babies in cradles. Angels hovering above the Earth, showering it with their benevolent light.

Sorrowmouth finally pricked at the woman's grief with his thorn until it seemed to bleed furious moonlight. Chaotic swirls of black and silver and red convulsing in the air around them. He gathered it all into his upturned bowl and began to sup at it like an eager dog.

Mary stubbed her cigarette out into an ashtray overflowing with them. Her eyes and face were wet with tears again. "They come to me," she said after a moment, her body turned now to Underhill's, so close that their knees were touching. She placed a hand on his and somehow, all the hardness went out of her face and she was only a woman lost in grief. All of the armour she wore out to the people on this estate had dropped away. "They come to me at night. When I'm in bed and I can't sleep. I think about them and they *come* to me." She smiled, her voice dropping to a whisper. "They lie down in bed with me and I don't feel so alone."

She glanced up at Underhill and she hesitantly put her hand on his face. Her fingers were rough. He could smell a lifetime of nicotine. She leaned forward and kissed him then. Her lips were softer than he'd expected. There was smoke in her breath. She withdrew after a moment. Whatever it was that had possessed her was satisfied and had moved on. "Look—" she said and reached into the pocket of her cardigan. She withdrew a long, perfectly white feather. "I found this one morning after they came to me. It was on the pillow."

There was nothing Underhill could say in view of that kind of evidence. They stayed like that for an hour or so, talking, sometimes kissing, sometimes drinking, until Sorrowmouth had had his fill. Mary's attention became hazy, diffuse. There was a lazy smile of bliss on her face because all of her sorrows had departed, if only for a short time. Around nine o'clock, she fell asleep and Underhill remained there, a stranger in her house, waiting for angels to arrive. Forty years and change, he'd been waiting. After a couple of hours he saw sense and covered her with a blanket. He made his way out quietly and went home.

Three

Varley lived in a faded Victorian house on a wide, tree-lined street in Bohemia. Although it was almost midnight, the heat had kept people up. He could hear the neighbours in their back yard, talking and laughing, the clink of wine glasses. Underhill's ancient motor-home sat on Varley's narrow drive, coated in several years worth of accrued grime. You could barely see in any of the windows. Step inside and you were confronted with the pathetic sum total of Underhill's possessions. He kept the tyres pumped up, drove it around the area a couple of times a month to keep the battery from going flat.

The facade of Varley's house was faded and peeling. Outside the door a plastic box was filled to the brim with empty wine bottles. A mine-field of cat shit. All of the strays in the neighbourhood gravitated to Varley; his deficiencies with social interaction did not extend to animals, so they travelled from miles around to drink his milk and eat the cheap food he left out for them. Then they crapped on his property and left. The parallels one could make with his human relationships was not readily apparent to him.

Underhill had forgotten his key again, rang the bell and waited. "Oh, hello, Underhill," Varley said, eventually peering around the front door. "It's a touch late, isn't it? Wasn't expecting you to come home tonight."

The two men stared at each other for a moment before discomfiture forced Varley's hand and he reluctantly tugged the door open to allow Underhill in. He'd all but lived here for the last six years and still they went through this preposterous charade every time Underhill came home late, or even the following day. They'd never agreed on the terms of their relationship; neither of them could really say what it was they wanted from the other. But Varley had always tried to make sure he felt significantly more than just a lodger.

Varley didn't wait for Underhill to close the door before shuffling away down a narrow hall piled on either side with newspapers and Sunday supplements going back several years. Underhill shrugged off his coat and hung it on his usual hook, dropped the rucksack at his feet. Sorrowmouth stared balefully at him for a moment on the doorstep, then lowered his head and ducked beneath the doorframe, squeezed his bulk into the hall.

Varley was in the kitchen, frozen for a moment, watching a large moth batting itself against the bare light bulb above his head. The walls and linoleum seemed to be saturated with several lifetimes of grease accrual. Beyond the windows was the remnant of an ancient wooden frame conservatory, built by Varley's father in the sixties, and subsequently abandoned by Varley in the nineties when the garden grew so unruly that he could no longer physically make his way into it anymore. A wall of tangled vines and brambles seemed to heave and groan beyond the kitchen windows like something from a John Wyndham novel. After a moment, Varley roused himself from his moth-induced stupor and said, "Where are my manners, Underhill? How about a cup of tea?"

"Thank you," Underhill said and sat down at the ancient pitted kitchen table. He could sense Sorrowmouth hovering in the doorway with his thorn and dish, scrutinising Varley with the kind of attentiveness the stray cats gave the various plates of cheap food that sat along the perimeter of the room. Underhill had had his fill of Sorrowmouth today. Too many years together in the same rooms; every day he ended up in this frazzled, fractious mood with no egress from the life they had shared these past 40 years. After a moment, Underhill watched him lumber away impatiently, to go foraging in Varley's cluttered rooms for stale fragments of misery. By now he knew where Varley went to drown his sorrows, vent his frustrations.

"Did you see they had a jumper at Beachy Head last night?" Varley said, his back to Underhill as he arranged the chipped mugs and boiled the kettle.

"Really?" Underhill said. "It's hardly news now, is it?"

Varley chanced a glance over his shoulder at Underhill. "No, I suppose not. Except the woman involved survived."

Underhill had had his fill of death for one day, but that piqued his interest. "How the devil did she manage that?"

Varley shrugged, distracted by the moth again. "She was lucky, I suppose." After a moment's reflection, he added: "Although I suspect she probably doesn't see it that way."

Later Underhill watched the local news on Varley's iPad. A reporter stood on the blustery headland, the sea rolling in frothing white waves behind him.

"During the course of a year over a million people will walk this stretch of East Sussex coastline. Beachy Head has gained a reputation as a place of outstanding natural beauty. However it's also gained another one: that of being a place where some people come to end their lives.

"In fact, the chalk sea cliff in Eastbourne is one of the most notorious suicide spots in the world, beside San Francisco's Golden Gate Bridge and the Aokigahara Woods in Japan. The Beachy Head Chaplaincy Team conducts regular patrols of the area in a bid to locate and halt potential cliff jumpers." The reporter's hair whipped in the stiff breeze coming off the sea. "There are also multiple signs posted with the telephone number for the Samaritans, urging potential jumpers to call them.

"The woman leapt from Sugar Lump cliff here on Beachy Head," the reporter continued. "75 feet into the fall she was caught by some extending rocks. After a few hours she was heard crying out by a local resident, walking his dogs."

One of the Eastbourne RNLI was interviewed. "When we got the call I thought we'd be looking for a body," the man said. His face looked like it had been carved out of the chalky cliffs. His brow was heavy and his eyes half given over to the sea. "We conducted a shoreline search when our crew heard the woman shouting and waving down to us."

"The woman," the reporter said, "has been taken to hospital where she will be monitored for the next few days."

Underhill hadn't noticed until after the report that Varley had taken hold of his hand. When he glanced across, Varley offered him a smile so benevolent it almost broke him.

"I know it's the anniversary tomorrow," he said softly. "I know it must be hard. You shouldn't keep obsessing about these things."

After all this time, all the years that Underhill had neglected the feelings of this kind, reticent man, Varley could still find it in himself to reach out and offer him comfort. But Underhill didn't crave sympathy. It had happened so long ago it almost didn't feel like it applied to him anymore. And he honestly believed that he didn't deserve Varley's benign generosity. He withdrew his hand and they didn't speak about the matter again.

Later, in bed, Varley went through the motions of initiating some sort of sexual contact and, after some reluctance, Underhill simply welcomed the other man into his arms and left all that straining and grunting to younger men than themselves. After a while he heard Varley begin to snore and lay there, picturing the woman at the precipice of the cliff top, at the moment of leaving the world by leaping into it, and wondered what her reasons might be; perhaps no one save for her loved ones would ever know.

Sorrowmouth squatted in the corner of the room, an ugly colossus with his shoulders thrust into the eaves. Underhill listened to the flea breathing, his mass stilling in the darkness. They stared at each other for some time until sleep finally claimed them both.

Four

Underhill had worked for almost thirty years in domestic services at the local hospital in Hastings. He'd been there longer than almost anyone in the entire facility, content to remain in a position that offered less than minimum wage, cleaning wards, beds, corridors and toilets, keeping his head down for eight hours a day and then going home. It satisfied him to never really rise above what he considered his station in life. Underhill had no qualms about the inequalities and lack of opportunities for a man with a comprehensive school education and no qualifications.

The job had suited Underhill and Sorrowmouth well. While Underhill kept his head down, Sorrowmouth would roam around him, feeding on all manner of fresh grief and panic and fear. Each day his bowl would be filled to the brim. But then, after almost thirty years, the manager of domestic services had called Underhill into his office and all but insisted that he take the position of supervisor. It took him off the floor and into an office, arranging rotas and controlling budgets and recruiting and training staff. Nonetheless, Sorrowmouth remained free to sit nearby, occasionally making a foray into accident and emergency, where the mood was often fraught and filled with opportunities to feed. Underhill had settled into the role quickly. There was a little more money in his pocket, and the day was certainly less back-breaking.

That day he was scheduled to spend the first few hours conducting interviews for two new assistant positions. Even with his window open the heat gathered quickly, leaving Underhill short-tempered and uncomfortable. His thoughts kept coming back around to his mother. The anniversary of her death. Later, after a cigarette break he discovered that the woman who'd jumped from Beachy Head had been brought here. She had her own room, more out of luck than any other reason. Underhill knew Poppy, one of the nurses on the ward and asked after the woman.

"How is she?" he asked.

"The jumper?" Poppy said, her face flushed. "She's all right, all things considered. No broken bones, just a few cuts and bruises." She shook her head. "75 feet down, though. That's *crackers*. Charmed life to survive that, I reckon."

Underhill glanced through the open door at the woman in the bed. She was asleep, her face turned away to the quivering light from the open window. A slight woman in her forties, a mass of blonde curls on the pillow. "What do you think will happen to her?"

"There's a mental health worker due later this afternoon to assess her."

"Will they section her?"

"I doubt it. She was a bit distressed when she came in. She kept saying something about – what was it, now? – Prurience. Something about being too far from prurience." She shook her head. "Isn't that something about dirty thoughts or something?"

Underhill peered into the room, at each of the corners. There was nothing there. "I really wouldn't know," he said finally and left the woman to sleep.

Five

Underhill's old man owned a sad little second-hand bookshop on Queen's Road, five minutes from the promenade and lost among a sea of kebab houses, dry-cleaners and betting shops. It had once been a Blockbuster video store and still bore the old colours and faded company markings. With a thrifty eye for signage, the old man had called the store Bookbuster and painted in the new letters himself. Books long faded by the sun were piled up in the dusty window beside old signs offering transfer of VHS, slides and cinefilm onto DVD. There were wooden boxes outside with damp vinyl records and ancient seaside postcards from another era.

Underhill found the old man buried in an alcove at the back of the narrow store, behind a mountain of remaindered stock and second-hand hardbacks gone yellow with age. Landslides at every turn. You navigated your way to the back of the store like it was a labyrinth but the old man waiting there for you behind a wall of books and ancient cassettes was a slightly pathetic Minotaur in exchange for your troubles.

He was distracted with an old mono copy of Rubber Soul. He was holding it to the light of an ancient angle poise lamp, a cigarette gripped between his cracked lips. He had a shock of wild grey hair and thick black spectacles. A long, dirty looking beard. A loose green cardigan hung off him. There was less and less of him every time Underhill visited.

After a moment of intense scrutiny, he slid the record back into its sleeve and placed it down by his feet and only then glanced up, knocking over an old china cup in the process. It was filled with cigarette butts. His features knitted together for a moment and then he said: "Hello, boy. Wasn't expecting you."

"I was in the area," Underhill said. He glanced back to see Sorrowmouth straining his bulk through the door and attempting to navigate his way towards them. When he turned back, the old man was on his feet, looking in the same direction, his face unreadable.

"I'll close for lunch," he said and stepped over a mound of mouldy cardboard boxes marked *Dirty magazines – Penthouse, Playboy, Mayfair.*

Underhill always came away from here needing to shower. There was a lifetime of rot working its way through the bones of the building. Wallpaper peeling with black mould, bookcases heaving with books you couldn't even access; everything, including the old man, faded to the grey of ash.

"*Oi*," the old man said to a customer Underhill couldn't even see. "We're closing. Fuck off for half an hour, there's a good lad, eh?"

A moment later, Underhill saw a little man in a purple anorak covered in badges scurry out of the door and down the street.

After the old man had bolted the front door, he navigated his way back to the counter. He led Underhill up a narrow staircase stacked with ancient Penguin paperbacks. Underhill's heavy boots sounded impossibly loud on the bare wooden steps. The old man heaved, his lungs rattling as he reached the top. The landing smelled of mould, the floorspace narrowed with books that towered to head height on either side.

This was the inevitable end of the road for Underhill's old man. Maureen, his second wife, had died on Boxing Day last year. She had left him nothing in the will. Her sons had booted the old man out on his arse, so he'd gathered his belongings and retreated to this miserable little warren of rooms which got smaller every time new stock arrived. The greyness of it all; the windows choked with grime and discoloured net curtains. Thin threadbare carpet, ashtrays everywhere, filled with years of cigarettes. Dust suspended in the air.

"Is it that time of year again already?" The old man threw an old cat onto the rug and sat down heavily in his chair beside the two bar heater he called a fireplace. "We can't go a year without you coming around here to make me feel like shit for what happened, can we?"

Underhill noticed the black eye the old man was sporting, a long purple rain cloud, stretched across his cheek bone. By the chair was a cork board with a multitude of old photographs of Underhill's mother. Like a shrine. Every time he came here, the old man seemed to have found fresh evidence in the case for his defence. Black and white pictures of husband and wife as teenagers on the bonnet of an old Anglia, the old man with a gleaming back quiff and scuffed knuckles. Underhill's mother with the haunted look he'd become all too familiar with in the years of her absence. The old man had put that look there; day by day he'd chipped away at her resolve, her sense of identity, until all that was left was to persist, to endure the marriage before she found a way out.

"How did you get the black eye?" Underhill asked.

The old man pressed a finger to the bruise. "As if you give a shit."

Underhill smiled. "I really fucking don't."

"Maureen's sons," the old man said. "I went back to her house. *Our* bloody house. Left some things there that I wanted back. I let myself in one night and decided to kip there. It's just sitting empty. It's a fucking waste of a good bed until the place goes up for sale. Anyway, they found me in the morning, and promptly chucked me out on my ear."

Underhill didn't say anything. He'd never met Maureen. He'd seen her once or twice over the years but he had no insight into their marriage. But the fact that she'd left the old man nothing in her will spoke volumes.

"Why do you keep coming here, boy?" the old man asked.

"I don't know."

"Yes, you damn well do."

Underhill shrugged.

"If you're concerned that I'll forget, you shouldn't be." He glanced at the photos again, traced a broken yellow fingernail against the outline of her face. "What else do I have left to do? Now Maureen's gone, no fucker in their right mind would want me."

Underhill didn't respond. The old man stared at him, then hissed through his nose. He rooted through his pockets for his packet of cigarettes, and lit one. "Are we going to go around the houses again, boy? Like we always do?"

The first time, Underhill was six. He'd woken up in a wet bed. He kept doing it. His mother would quietly bathe him and put the sheets in for washing, never a raised voice, just the comfort of her smell, like freshly cut lavender, and then her warm embrace to say there was no harm done. Then one day the old man had gone upstairs to wake him for school and found the soaking wet sheets. Underhill still recalled a fleeting moment of white hot rage which seemed to fill the old man up like electricity. Underhill had shrunk back into the bed, terrified witless. At the last moment some misgiving washed over his father and instead he dragged Underhill from his bed and down the stairs and out of the house. Stiff with rage he marched his child down the street, barefoot in his wet pyjamas, past neighbours and school friends until he was red with shame. It was a dismal Tuesday morning in February. Rain in the air, the clouds flooding the sky.

"This will learn you a lesson, boy," the old man kept saying, as if to himself. "This will learn you."

Two streets away, three, four. Soon he was in an unfamiliar neighbourhood. He'd been reluctant as a child to stray too far from his mother's side, so he had no more than a handful of friends at school, certainly no one who Underhill would visit on different streets. He cried sometimes in school because he missed his mother and the comforts of his bedroom, or simply sitting in front of the TV beside the fire. When his father was away during the daytime the home felt more like *his* home; just Underhill and his mum. He'd always seen his father as a false note in the story of his life; as if they'd cast the wrong actor as his mother's husband: a coarse, violent man whose innate wit and intelligence had been dulled by years of hard drinking. Sometimes it would float to the surface, that different man, the one his mother had married; a man who read voraciously and would quote passages from his favourite poems by Philip Larkin or Carol Ann Duffy; a man who used to draw landscapes and buildings in fine spidery lines in a small hardbound book he kept in the pocket of every jacket he wore; a man who talked with a fiery passion about them emigrating to Italy to live off the land in Tuscany. But this man? This man didn't fit in their lives at all.

By the time they came to a sudden standstill Underhill was utterly unfamiliar with his surroundings. His pyjamas were dry now from the crisp sea breeze whipping through the narrow avenues, his bare feet frozen, his toes bunched. He could still smell the piss on him. Humiliation flared through him like fireworks. For a moment, his father hesitated and Underhill looked up into his eyes, searching for some fragment of compassion. Instead there was only that all-too-familiar loose gaze, fixed on nothing, an incandescent rage behind everything, every movement. The stink of cigarettes and booze on his breath. A stranger. He saw nothing of other fathers in this man, no benevolence, no paternal love of any kind. Finally he exhaled and took hold of his boy's arm, held it up at an awkward angle until he cried out. "This will learn you, boy. No child of mine pisses the bed like a little, fucking…fucking…" He ran out of words and hissed in exasperation. Then he decided on a course of action, something that had likely been percolating in his mind for some time, some method of punishment for a child he saw precious little of himself in, and which led to the kind of thoughts no man like himself should have to have: that perhaps this timid little boy who didn't go outside and play sports with other children, who sat in the bath or on his bed with his face turned to the window with a dreamy look in his eyes might not in fact be *his* at all, and that his wife, who was *far* too pretty (it was a blessing and a curse that a man like him should have landed so attractive a woman) might have gone elsewhere for affection seven years ago. The vines from this seed of doubt had sprouted into every waking moment, every interaction he had with his wife and child. It was a suspicion that hardened occasionally to certainty in his mind. On these days he felt only revulsion at the sight of the pair of them; so much so he sometimes had to remove himself from the household should he lose control and give into temper.

Finally Underhill's father turned on his heel and strode away from his child, moving so fast that Underhill hesitated for a moment. Then he began to run after his father. He didn't recognise this neighbourhood, he hadn't kept track of the streets they'd taken to get here. But then the old man turned on him and the look of hostility on his face was enough to freeze Underhill in his tracks.

"*Stay* here!"

Underhill felt tears brimming in his eyes and then they were spilling down his cheeks. Shivering in the cold breeze. The grey sky was flooding all of the windows of the houses in this street, making them look vacant; he heard no children, no schoolyard cries, nor even the sound of the sea: his natural compass was entirely broken. He lowered his gaze to his feet and shook. He felt his father considering him for a moment, hesitating perhaps, but then he repeated himself. "Stay here. Don't follow me, you hear? Make your own fucking way home."

Underhill had to fight with himself to remain in place. But something was already changing inside him. Something that had become familiar in the last year or so. He could feel the world subtly reordering itself as his father walked away; that dreamy feeling that he sometimes had and couldn't explain, not even to himself, so certainly not to his mother or anyone else. But he couldn't acknowledge it right now; he was afraid that if he didn't know his way home, he might wander lost in unfamiliar neighbourhoods until the end of time; he might end up in a different country altogether. Soon Underhill couldn't even hear his father's footsteps but the panic subsided, and the world gradually began to settle around him, changing little by little, soft and gentle and pliant, like his mother's embrace. He could hear the insect drone of a languid summer day and the silence of a Christmas Eve wrapped in snow. It tranquillised him. He looked up to find the buildings were all changed and very distant from him, like looking through the wrong end of a telescope. They were lit up from within with an incandescent golden light. They were like cathedrals floating in a changed sky; all the dreamy colours of a place where words ran out and art took over. Underhill had felt this strange abstracted feeling before, sitting in his bedroom window. The world settling around him, quelling all of his fears and anxieties, then transforming itself into something beyond the immaculate. Underhill drifted through the endless avenues, suspended on washes of impasto and evanescent spirals of ecstasy, transported away from the fraught little island he'd found himself born on. The vaulted sky arched like a vast cathedral. Buildings dissolved and then knitted themselves back together in ever more complex variations. He floated, lost and alternating between rapture and fear. He saw giants made out of shimmering lights, kaleidoscopes and cascading sounds, striding through the vast endless avenues. Trees wove intricate lattices of branches around him and angels came to settle there, their wings folded stiffly behind them. The air buckled around them. They gave off a fierce ravaged beauty; they glowed from within. The sound they made was like an orchestra tuning up, rising in intensity, becoming eerie quavering falsettos. The universe opened its arms up to Underhill then and he was seized with a feeling of intense benevolence and belonging. There was a truth beyond his understanding at that moment, a mystery hiding at the heart of all things. Everything narrowed and intensified until it felt as if this rapture would fill him to the absolute brim and unmake the body he was born into.

Underhill's mother found him eventually, rousing him from his reverie when she clutched at him, gathered him up into her arms and that familiar smell of lavender that he adored so much. She took him home and gradually the strange visions of a world transformed faded away and all that was left was his house and his mother bathing him, keeping him home from school for the day. He heard her crying downstairs later. He didn't know how to comfort her. The world seemed full of sharp edges again, the centre of which eluded him. That other world felt sometimes like a poisoned chalice, a box full of darkness.

His father, a wholly unoriginal man, repeated the punishment frequently. Every time Underhill did something wrong he would march him away from their home, into unfamiliar neighbourhoods, and leave him there. It became something akin to a ritual for both of them; a bizarre father-son activity. Something about the emotions evoked by the discipline would leave Underhill floating in that odd, phantasmagorical state. He saw angels often, even when that transformed world receded. They clustered around the chimney pots of the old houses of the neighbourhood, or on streetlights fizzing with electricity, or on lonely railway station platforms, their beautiful wings outstretched, faces pale and unearthly and inscrutable.

At some point during one of these episodes he must have told his mother and father about the impossible city. He didn't explicitly remember when this was, but he recalled the peculiar, disconcerted look on his father's face. Nonetheless he persisted with the punishment. When Underhill was eight the old man bought an old Ford Cortina from one of the neighbours and began to take Underhill further afield, as if it had become a game of wits between them, taking the child further and further away so he'd never find his way home. The visions continued; his father would enquire sometimes about them, and listen with a curious detached look on his face, as if listening to the reports of some traveller in a distant land. It didn't matter how hard he looked, the transfigured landscape that his son travelled in would always elude him.

One day he told Underhill about William Blake. He had a couple of old hardback books, one containing poetry, one filled with paintings. He told Underhill about Blake as a child, seeing angels in the mulberry trees of Peckham Rye, seeing the face of God pressed to his window, which set him off screaming. "Blake didn't see all those stinking alleyways and streets, all the whores and the scavengers and the piss-covered cobblestones," he told Underhill in a strange lucid manner that unnerved the boy. "He saw a city illuminated with angels and prophets and God." He pulled the car to a halt in an industrial estate in Hollington. Underhill had waited for this unfamiliar eloquent man masquerading as his father to continue, to fill in the details of Blake, who saw the same things he saw, but the old man gripped the steering wheel, staring straight ahead until Underhill opened the door and got out. His father drove away then and Underhill watched him go.

A year later, when Underhill was nine, the old man began meting out the same punishment to his wife for obscurely considered misdemeanours. Even when he wasn't inebriated his judgement was flawed, and he began to believe that his wife was carrying on with other men: the milkman; the window cleaner; the man who ran the corner store; the neighbour's husband. One by one his drinking friends dropped away from him because of his violent temper at the end of the night; he became the self-consumer of his woes. No sense of life anymore; the dreams of youth in his notebooks burned on a fire in the back garden, as if to show God that all of that wasted ambition didn't affect him. All that was left was to alienate his family further, punish the boy for his visions and punish the woman who'd once loved him for no longer smiling or weeping or so much as *living* when she was close.

He began to put her in the car and drive her away from Hastings, sometimes to Brighton, or Winchelsea or Rye, and leave her there. Sometimes she would have her purse with her and be able to afford a train or a bus home; sometimes if she was empty handed she would have to phone her brother who lived in New Romney to pick her up and bring her home.

Then one bright day in July, after a particularly vicious row, the old man took his wife by the hair and dragged her down their garden path and bustled her into the Cortina. He drove her in silence to Eastbourne and out the other side, up onto Beachy Head Road where the land was suddenly very flat and the sky a huge blanket of blue, not a cloud to be seen. The fields were very green and the trees very still. Sheep and cows lying stunned in the gathering heat. Finally to the left the land fell away to reveal the vastness of the sea below them, the waves foaming on the shingle. It was early, there was no one yet parked in the carpark of the visitors centre. Just a couple of men, walking their dogs. Underhill's father parked the car and placed his hands on the wheel, his wife staring at him until all the emotions went away from her one final time. There was nothing familiar about him anymore; there was no longer any semblance of the young man she'd met when she was 16. Where once there had been vigour and ambition there was now only defeat and spite. He was not the man she'd once loved, so she got out of the car and waited for him to drive away.

Underhill didn't know much about the final moments of his mother's life. Had she thought of him? He supposed so; perhaps only him. There was probably still that turmoil about her decision as she made her way across the car park and through the long grass to the edge of the land. Had there been mobile phones back then, Underhill often wondered if she would have called him to explain her actions. Perhaps not; his voice might have been the only thing left to dissuade her from her actions.

It took her half an hour to decide on the location. She passed the warning signs and the crosses, half-buried in the ground. She stood at the edge of the cliff and considered the world spread out before her. Here perhaps she could place order on a life where there had been none, just the constant and unpredictable anxiety of what manner of conflict her husband would bring home with him each night. Here she could finally draw a line beneath it all. Here, she could take control of her life by taking it away from everyone else. From *him*, most of all, because he deserved it, a huge dose of what she'd come to accept, day by shitty day. She looked down at the shingle beach far below and swayed on rubber legs in the breeze; it was the only prompt she needed; she tumbled away from the edge and into space, screaming.

And so here they were, all these years later, Underhill inexplicably given to circling the man who'd tormented him as a child and sent his mother to her death. *Going around the houses. Like we always do.*

"I see another poor fucker tried to do it and survived," his father said. "Nothing worse than that. Fucking the whole thing up. Having to live when you don't fucking-well want to."

Even after all these years, both of them still keeping tabs on all the jumpers from Beachy Head. What purpose did it serve? "There are plenty of other ways," Underhill said. "If they want to end it."

"Not like that though. No need to save up your pills for a couple of months, or order a hose off eBay so you can attach to the exhaust in your garage. You just keep on walking. There's a *certainty* to that. There's fucking *poetry* to that, boy. You make your decision and you just keep on walking." The old man glanced again at the pictures beside him. He waved a hand, dismissively. "Into the air."

Why had he come here? Why did he *keep* coming here? Underhill felt it, that notion of it solidifying in his imagination in a way little else had for many years. The restlessness to his movements. He couldn't decide if it began in him or in Sorrowmouth. He hovered in the doorway, snorting through his nose, unwilling to move any closer to Underhill's old man. Underhill had explicitly stated that he was not to feed on him, no matter what kind of feast he'd find here in these pitiful surroundings. The old man didn't deserve that kind of relief. He had glanced once or twice in Sorrowmouth's direction; Underhill wasn't sure what he saw, if anything. Just the impression of something wholly unfamiliar to his estimation of the world.

"They keep going there, to Beachy Head, I mean, because of the poetry of it," the old man insisted, settling into a theory he'd expounded on more than once to Underhill. Sometimes he simply stared at this man, this terrible man, who'd made their lives a misery and effectively ended the life of the woman both of them had loved, and Underhill thought, *you deserve to rot slowly, alone and unloved*, and realised that, all these years since her death, he had. "It feeds off itself, doesn't it? The words they use. Calling it a suicide hotspot. And the national newspapers sensationalising it the way they do. The language of it is like a virus; it only makes it more appealing to that kind of person."

"'That kind of person.'" Underhill said it under his breath, his irritation growing.

"Like the sirens, calling out to them."

"I have something to tell you."

"Oh, yeah? Have you won the lottery? Are you going to treat me to a new house?"

"No," Underhill said. He swallowed, hesitated, glanced at Sorrowmouth, who stared back at him with that sour look on his face. "I'm going to kill myself," he said.

The old man simply stared at him. A stunned moment of silence. Then he said: "Don't be so fucking stupid."

"I mean it. You won't see me again. This is the last time."

There was a look of mounting consternation on the old man's face. He was wholly unprepared for this U-turn in their exchange.

"Is this to punish me?" The old man's dismay quickly turned to anger. It always had. All these years.

Underhill shook his head. "Who can say?"

"*Fuck off*, then," the old man spat from his threadbare chair, an accusatory finger piercing a wreath of cigarette smoke. He seemed much smaller now, like an ancient corpse, waiting for the grave. "Go and fucking follow her off a cliff." He turned away from Underhill then, dismissing him.

Underhill turned to go, shepherding Sorrowmouth back down the narrow staircase.

"Boy?"

Underhill turned, reluctantly. "Yes?" he said.

The old man's eyes were glassy. He stared at Underhill for a moment and then shook his head. "Nothing," he said.

Six

The next day Underhill encountered the jumper in the hospital cafe. It was a sad little space that Underhill rarely frequented, filled with the families of patients, their hands animated with the anticipation of whatever came next for their loved ones, whispering over bad coffee and emaciated cheese and onion sandwiches that they only ever picked at, leaving the bright rings of onion on their plate, untouched. Sorrowmouth liked it here. It was close to Underhill's office; he came down here to eat too; he, however, never wasted a drop.

Underhill recognised the woman immediately. Blonde curls and a look of haunted stillness. She seemed to be absorbing all of the light from the room, pushing people away with the certainty of her deed, the absolute clarity of it, still radiating in waves of anger and frustration and sorrow. A tightly packed rose in the same long, out of shape pullover that she'd leapt from the cliff in. There was a tear in the knee of her jeans. Underhill idly wondered if she'd torn them in the fall or they were artfully ripped. He hesitated at the entrance to the cafe and finally decided to step inside before he drew attention to himself. He bought a coffee and sat one table away from the woman. He chanced another glance at her; she was picking at her lip repetitively, allowing her curls to fall across her scratched face. She seemed in a state of vague agitation; Underhill wondered how the mental health worker had allowed her to walk away from here without thinking she'd go right back to Beachy Head to finish the job.

When she looked up suddenly, he was unprepared. She smiled at him, lifting her right arm, which was bandaged from wrist to elbow, as if to say: *I tossed myself off Beachy Head and all I got was this lousy bandage!* Underhill smiled back and began to speak but she was looking past him, beyond the entrance, where Sorrowmouth squatted in a square of brilliant light that turned the ridges of his spinal column a burnished gold. The smile fell from her lips. Underhill glanced at Sorrowmouth and then back to the woman. Something fell into place. She spread her fingers out on the table as if to prove that everything else about the world was in its correct place and that nothing had come undone in her mind. Satisfied she said in no more than a whisper: "Does that belong to you?"

"Yes," Underhill said.

She nodded. "And no one else can see it."

"No. No one else."

"Did you know *I* would be able to?"

"I don't know. Maybe. I don't know why."

She studied Underhill's face, looking for all the ways men had failed her over the years, but you couldn't see the future, no matter how hard you looked, so she let it go. "I'm Catherine," she said. "But Kate. People call me Kate."

"My name is William," Underhill said. "And that's Sorrowmouth."

She let out a quick, startled laugh. "How did you decide what to call it?"

"I don't really know, to tell you the truth," Underhill said. "He's been with me since I was ten. At first he was just 'the flea' but then I just started thinking of him as Sorrowmouth one day and it became a habit."

"The flea?"

"It's a long story."

She nodded. "Prurience," she said. "I call mine Prurience."

"Where is it?"

"I don't know. I assume she's waiting for me nearby." She paused for a moment. "I jumped from Beachy Head the other day."

"I know. I saw it on the news," Underhill said. "Was Prurience there too?"

"I told her she couldn't jump too. '*Don't you dare!*' I said. I didn't want her following me into the next life." She laughed at that. "Next life. Christ."

"Aren't you in pain? Being this far apart from her."

"Not really. I think they gave me morphine. It's nice. I still can't feel a thing."

"But there's that umbilical cord thing, isn't there? Being apart, it hurts."

"You have that too?"

He nodded.

"You're the first," she said. "I've never met anyone else with one of those things."

"Nor me. Lucky us."

"Yes. Look how happy we are about it." She scratched at the skin beneath the bandage. "I'd have preferred a cat, to be brutally fucking honest."

Underhill smiled. He liked her. It felt novel to smile, to have such a sudden shared intimacy with someone without having to take his clothes off. "Do you think she stayed there, at Beachy Head?" he asked.

"Christ knows. That's a long bus journey from here just to find out."

"You're not intending to go back?"

She smiled and ran a fingernail into the indentation of someone's name on the table. "No," she said, almost shyly. "No, I don't think so." She looked at Underhill, into his eyes, looking for something that he feared he may not have to give.

"Not yet," she said.

Seven

Things fell apart quickly after the death of Underhill's mother.

At some point she had contacted Social Services, made enquiries about what kind of protection they could offer her child should something happen to her. After her suicide a social worker arrived on the doorstep one day, quietly but firmly suggesting they needed to sit down with Underhill's father and then Underhill himself afterwards. The old man was sober enough that day, but the social worker came away with some concerns and decided that Underhill was a child in need and arranged a child protection conference. There were, he said, concerns about Underhill's welfare following his mother's death and clear signs of domestic abuse. Underhill frequently sported bruises along his arms where the old man took hold of him, yanking him down the garden path and into the car. He didn't hit him; he was aware that there were bruises that could be explained away and some that couldn't. The social worker attempted to go through his prepared notes prior to the conference but the old man didn't want to know; during a rare lucid day he sat down and wrote an eloquent essay about his life with and without his darling wife and what kind of support he felt he needed. He arrived at the conference in his best suit, shaved and clean and sober. Underhill getting a rare glimpse of whatever it was his mother had seen in him all those years ago. He presented himself well, and suggested that things had been fraught in the months leading up to his wife's suicide; the notes he presented suggested that much of the problem was her deteriorating mental health. Nonetheless a child protection plan was drawn up and a key social worker was allocated to Underhill and a further review suggested within six months.

The old man drove Underhill home in silence. Then he left him there and went to get pissed. Underhill didn't see him for three days.

Early one morning, two months later, Underhill let himself into the room where his old man kept his books. A narrow room at the back of the house, the walls crowded with old hardbacks and paperbacks, and with a well worn armchair beside a small fireplace. He knew what he was looking for. While the old man was asleep he crept in with a can of cola he'd found at the back of the fridge. Beside 'Pale Fire' and 'News from Nowhere' there were two volumes by William Blake on the shelves. The battered Penguin Classics paperback of Blake's complete poems didn't hold Underhill's attention for long; he flipped back and forth through the thin pages looking for mentions of angels in the trees and God at the window, but quickly grew exasperated with it. He carefully placed it back on the shelf and instead withdrew the other, larger volume, 'William Blake: Masterpieces of Art'. It was immediately more appealing. There was a small writing desk placed in the corner of the room with a window that offered a view of the back garden, now sliding into wild neglect after his mother's death. Underhill placed the book down on here, along with his can of cola, moving aside his father's recent acquisitions from the second-hand bookshop he would ultimately take over the lease of some twenty years later. In recent days he'd sat in here, struggling with 'Finnegan's Wake,' several times swearing in frustration at the book. In his younger days Underhill's father had sat at this battered desk with his pen and his journals, sometimes even a typewriter, staring out into his new garden while his wife hung washing on the line, and fancy himself some burgeoning Dylan Thomas, the 'roistering, drunken and doomed poet.' But everything was a fragment of a frustrated whole, unfinished, tossed in the bin, burned in a fire outside. If the muses would not bend to his will then he'd burn the whole lot to spite them for their constant disregard.

Underhill leafed through the pages, drawn to 'The Angels Hovering over the Body of Christ in the Sepulchre'. These angels, with their wings stretched high above them, unsettled him; he'd seen them on the rooftops of this town and in the impossibly delicate latticework of trees in the other world. The sense of something he thought he owned solely having been traversed and mapped and documented a hundred years before his birth felt curiously like a secret spoiled. The accompanying text described Blake at the age of eight, telling his mother he had seen a tree full of angels "bespangling every bough like stars". The naked figures in 'The Dance of Albion' and the illustrations from Milton's 'Paradise Lost' stirred other feelings in him that he had yet to put a name to. The golden light of the city of floating cathedrals was prevalent everywhere. It seemed to consolidate all of Underhill's misgivings about his visions; it conferred to him that others had seen the world he'd wandered in, others had reported back and made art to pay obeisance to its glory. The initial disappointment that he was not a pioneer was tempered by the thrill of knowing that he was not alone, that he was not entirely mad.

Another painting caught Underhill's eye that morning. It was a curious, seductive illustration. 'The Ghost of a Flea'. A grotesque naked colossus, at odds with the suggestion of its tiny incarnation as insect, stalking through a starry realm between stage curtains, almost as if treading the boards of a theatre stage. This ghost didn't seem to suggest a flea of any kind to Underhill; it was mad-eyed and bestial, its tongue pointed and voracious, the hard long curve of spine like a throbbing column of glistening bone. In one hand the creature had a peculiar curved knife that looked like a thorn to Underhill, and in the other a stone bowl. All Underhill knew of fleas were that they feasted on blood; it struck him momentarily that this peculiar giant would in similar parasitical manner use the thorn to prick at its victims and collect the blood in its bowl. He had no concept that Blake might have considered this ghost of a flea as if through a magnifying glass and not the giant he first appeared to be.

Blake, Underhill read, had claimed he was 'visited' by the entity, who posed for him as he sketched it. He was able to communicate with the monstrous being, who revealed that all fleas were inhabited by the souls of men who were 'by nature bloodthirsty to excess'. There was further debate in the text about Jungian archetypes, religious visions and hallucinations borne of a mental illness, but then Underhill heard the sound of his father approaching. In his alarm at being discovered he knocked his half-full can of cola across the desk. It quickly soaked the volume of Blake's art, transforming 'The Ghost of a Flea' into a dirty brown stain. Underhill could feel the panic stiffening his bones. He didn't know what to do. His father flung open the door, and saw Underhill at the desk with his book, and the mess that he'd made of it. He'd just risen; his hair was awry and his eyes were already wild with anger. There was nowhere for Underhill to run. As his father rushed towards him, he recoiled into the corner of the room, his hands sticky from trying to brush the cola from the book. He didn't hear his father's words; they were mostly expletives. His rage was out of all proportion. For a moment all that Underhill saw was Blake's flea lumbering towards him with the thorn and the bowl, eager for blood as penance for a ruined book.

Underhill didn't recall anything immediately beyond that point. The next solid memory was waking up in hospital, several days later. According to the doctor, his father claimed his son had fallen and struck his head. An ambulance had been called when Underhill had suffered what was to be the first of several seizures. He'd suffered a skull fracture and a small right frontal lobe contusion, which the doctor described as a bruise on Underhill's brain. He had come around under admission to the hospital, only to be confused and combative and requiring sedation. The hospital placed Underhill on medication to prevent further seizures, which might worsen brain swelling.

Underhill's father wasn't there when he woke up. He wasn't there later either. No one would tell him why. Instead the nurses mothered him a bit and he lapped up the attention. He had a bandaged head; he felt like a survivor of the war. A few days later his maternal grandmother arrived. She was a gentle woman, similar in temperament to her departed daughter. She had the same kind eyes that suggested limitless patience, a boundless capacity for love. She told him that his father would not be coming to see him in the near future. The hospital had gathered photographs, x-rays and scans and notes, then brought in Underhill's social worker, who'd contacted the police in response to the evidence that the hospital had compiled. The local authority then issued an application for an Emergency Protection Order. The case came to court the next day. A judge made a decision based on the evidence and ruled that Underhill would not be returned to his father, and would instead, for the interim, be placed in his grandparents' care. Underhill didn't recall or properly comprehend the event that had caused this furore in the adults' world, but welcomed the opportunity to not go home. But then a couple of months after being discharged, Underhill experienced his next seizure. It started while he was in school: a minor jerking in his left arm, then losing his balance, collapsing on the playground and convulsing. It lasted for a minute or so; he didn't recall any of it, save for coming round with a circle of children and teachers standing over him. He was taken to hospital again and there was another battery of tests. Finally he was released again with medication for the epilepsy.

Then, not long after, he woke one night in the narrow spare room in his grandparents' house and sensed someone else in the room with him. He stirred quickly, alarmed that it might be his father, who'd quickly attained the status of bogeyman due to the vagueness of what had happened that day, and the hushed whispers his grandparents spoke in when they mentioned him.

But it wasn't his father. It was the thing from Blake's painting. The Ghost of a Flea. It sat squashed in the corner of the room with its scaly muscular knees pushed up beneath its stubby chin, its shoulder hunched against the ceiling. Its head was too small for the grotesque bulk of its body. Its skin glowed in the dark like burnished gold. Underhill stared through the gloom at the naked interloper, curious at how unafraid he felt. It was mute but seemed to simmer with an unreleasable tension, the air between them fraught with something Underhill struggled to grasp that first night, and for many years afterward. A black and silver cloud of matter seemed to flood the air around it, like a Pollack painting come to life. The flea clenched its teeth together like an ape and used the thorn in its clawed hands to probe at the yellow and brown deposits on their surface. The bowl sat at its feet, empty and expectant. It wouldn't be until Underhill was in the first flush of adolescence that the flea became his constant companion and the empty bowl became the symbol of their power struggle. That first night it stared balefully at Underhill until, satisfied that this colossal thing was of no immediate harm to him, he fell back asleep.

It became *he*. *He* became Sorrowmouth.

Sorrowmouth continued to sit in every narrow abode that Underhill chose to call home. He even – just about – fitted his bulk inside the knackered old motorhome parked on Varley's drive. He watched him shit and sleep and fuck and bathe. He followed him to every lover's house, every pub he sat in, every dentist appointment he attended.

Initially Underhill brought it water and juice and tea; he even on his fourteen birthday made a small cut in his finger and allowed the blood to dribble into the wooden bowl. Sorrowmouth looked down at the paltry offering with a look of mild distaste. Finally he pressed the lip of the bowl to his pointed tongue, and after a moment's contemplation, shook his head.

Later that year, Underhill's father was charged with child cruelty and neglect. Social services could not prove that he had struck Underhill or used excessive force on the day of his hospitalisation, although almost everyone was convinced that the severity of the injury could not have been caused in any other way. The court imposed a two-year custodial sentence, necessitating the old man to be subject to a curfew, to undertake a treatment programme for alcohol, and be subject to a rehabilitation activity. He wasn't allowed any access to his son. It didn't affect Underhill at all; a deep-seated loathing had gradually settled into his bones for the man. He was happier with his grandparents in that narrow spare room, which they'd filled with all of his things.

It took some time for Underhill to comprehend that the visions had gone. He realised one day in the middle of summer that he hadn't been visited by angels or walked in floating cathedrals in cities made of gold since before the hospital, before the epilepsy. It had all been exchanged for the flea – Blake's beautiful visions withdrawn and replaced with one of his most nightmarish. It seemed like a poor exchange. Underhill longed for those exultant visions; and then, when he was sure that they would not return, he mourned them. He took out a volume of Blake's paintings from the library and studied them again without fear of reprisal. It didn't bring the visions back. It was hard to accept the loss of that impossible place and the rapturous feeling of contentment it had offered. The mystery that lay packed in the heart of tightly packed rose would forever elude him. A box full of darkness was all he had left.

And then his grandmother died and Underhill realised what it was that the flea expected of him.

Eight

Later, Underhill drank alone in his favourite pub in Bohemia village. The local ales were good and he could spend half an hour feeding money into the jukebox, listening to songs that seemed to cut to the quick of the confusion of his feelings. Sorrowmouth squatted in a corner beside the pool table, speculatively watching two old men at the end of the bar, one of them crying into a large handkerchief, the other trying his best to support him. Underhill hadn't planned to tell his old man about his intentions. The thing that had only been notional in his mind felt more like a solid thing, a manifesto that he now felt bound to act upon. It didn't scare him; the seed of it had been sown all those years ago when his mother had seen no other option but to throw herself off Beachy Head; if anything it felt strangely like resolution, like the only answer to the questions he'd been asking himself for almost forty years. By the time he made his way down the street and let himself into Varley's house, he was half-cut and sweating from the walk home, pointedly aware that the apple had not fallen far from the tree.

He said Varley's name several times, moving slowly through the rooms, pressing his hands against the scuffed walls as they spun gently away from him. When he didn't find his lover downstairs, he knew all too well where he'd be and hesitated as he always did.

He stood at the bottom of the staircase and peered into the early evening gloom, the sweat drying on his skin.

He discovered Varley in Annabel's room. Nothing left in there – no furniture, no carpet, no toys, no books, no daughter. Varley was stood in an oblique square of light as it fled the day, looking misplaced, like he was convinced that this room was a portal to another, simpler time, only to ever find it empty and his daughter forever absent. He turned to Underhill and offered a wretched smile. Varley was a man wholly sensitive to the vicissitudes of others, often to the detriment of his own feelings and needs. Even in pain, as he was every time he stepped over the threshold to his daughter's room, he would abandon his own distress if he thought it made others uncomfortable. Underhill knew he came to stand in here at night, long after he should have been asleep. On occasion Underhill would find him curled up on the bare wooden floorboards. He would bring a pillow and place it gently beneath his head, cover him with a blanket.

"Underhill," he said. "Sorry, I didn't hear you come in."

"Don't," Underhill said, raising a hand to him before he abandoned the room. "I'm pissed and I've had a difficult day. Best if I sleep it off."

"Let me make you a coffee," Varley said.

"No."

"Tea, then?"

"Thank you, but no." Underhill felt a surge of overwhelming guilt. It almost brought him to his knees. "Stay here. Stay with Annabel." He heard himself say her name and realised his error. There was a long, painful silence.

"It's not like she's here, is it?" Varley said finally.

Underhill felt the weight of the other man's grief, but his limbs were leaden and his head was pounding. "No," he said. He had to look away from Varley's face. Look too long and that kind of sorrow could break you in half. "I'm sorry," he began, but he didn't know how to continue. "I'm sorry that you got rid of all her things."

Varley looked baffled. "Why? That wasn't your fault. It was mine. I thought I was ready."

The rooms had stilled now. All that Underhill felt was fatigued by all these little routines they went through because of Sorrowmouth, because of the baggage he brought to every room he'd walked into for the last forty-odd years. It exhausted him. He was tired of not being the person they thought he was, tired of letting them down. "No," he said finally. He hesitated with the words but then there was only the truth. "It is my fault. *It is*. You were still grieving that first time we ran into each other. You were at your wit's end. You'd just lost your daughter. Your *wife* had left you, for God's sake."

"And I met *you*," Varley said, with an exaggerated levity that had once been a lover's joke but now simply sounded like he was taking the piss. "I was… I was dead inside when I met you, William. You must remember that." They never called each other by their christian names, only when they were both drunk, or very, very sad.

"I do," Underhill said. "I remember it clearly. I'm glad. I'm glad that you managed to find your way back to living again."

"But that was *you*, William. You must know that you were the reason for that."

"It wasn't me," Underhill said. "You just thought it was."

Varley looked bewildered. Neither of them had expected to speak this way. It was the booze, Underhill supposed; it was the sure knowledge that he wanted to leave – not just this man and his almost limitless patience and belief in him, but this world and what he'd made of his time in it.

"If it wasn't you who made me feel like a human being again, then who was it?"

Underhill hesitated. How to make him understand after all this time? "Do you remember when you met me?"

"Of course I do. You were laying flowers by the roadside down the street. Everyone came to leave something after Annabel died."

"I didn't have flowers," Underhill said. "You just assumed it was why I was there. You were, I don't know, mad with grief. You didn't know which way was up. It was easy to make that mistake."

Varley took a moment to assimilate that information. He remained in the centre of the room, as the last of the light crept away from the windows and into the horizon. "So why were you there?"

Underhill looked at Varley, then away. He'd started to slide down the door frame, as if he was collapsing upon himself. He had no strength left. "Sorrowmouth," he said finally.

"Sorrow what?"

"I don't think I can make you understand," Underhill said.

Varley squinted through the encroaching gloom at a man he was fast losing sight of; a man who was becoming a stranger again. "*Try,*" he said. "Try to make me understand."

Underhill rubbed at his head with both hands, attempting to find the words. "I came to the roadside memorial for the sorrow. It's what I do. I don't want to. It's just that I've had no other choice for a very long time. Imagine how much grief and pain is in the air around those places where people have died. Imagine how much bloody *mourning* people bring to those places."

"It was where we found her," Varley said. "An accident. When we got there the man who'd hit her was sitting by the side of the road crying. I've never seen anyone so upset. And then I saw her."

Underhill closed his eyes. He felt his throat swelling. "I know," he said.

Annabel had run out into the road that afternoon and the man, a father of three himself, hadn't seen her. He'd been going a few miles over the speed limit. Varley had never really blamed him. Later he discovered that his marriage too had crumbled into nothing in the aftermath. Two different types of grief, bonded by the death of one little girl. Annabel had gone under the wheels somehow and died instantly. She was at the side of the road when Varley and his wife found her and the driver. He'd phoned for an ambulance before they arrived. Varley's little girl had died in his arms.

The place sang out from miles away. Underhill and the flea had trekked here six years ago so Sorrowmouth could fill his bowl with a grief that had flooded the entire area, a black and silver maelstrom in the air that only Underhill could see. He'd crouched to pick up some flowers he'd noticed in the road and when he looked up, there was Varley in last week's clothes, his hair uncombed, with a look so desolate it took

Underhill aback. He was crazed with grief. "Thank you," he had said to Underhill, solicitous even in the depths of torment. "I'm sorry, have we met?"

Sorrowmouth waded through the clouds of anguish, immediately drawn to this lighthouse of misery, this nucleus of pain, while Underhill struggled with an appropriate fabrication. "No, but I live nearby," he'd said finally. "I was so sorry to hear about your loss. I can't imagine how you must be feeling."

"My wife left me today," Varley had said, as if he was sharing small-talk about the weather.

"Oh," Underhill said. "I'm sorry."

Sorrowmouth had stood poised with his thorn and dish, having come to learn that life was easier with affirmation from Underhill in these matters. Underhill could not think of one thing to say to ease this wretched man's suffering, so instead he nodded and Sorrowmouth pricked at the turbulent starburst of reds and yellows, greys and browns that swirled around him. They began to convulse and gather together, sliding like liquid down a plughole into Sorrowmouth's upturned bowl. And, as the air began to clear around Varley, Underhill saw something of the man he'd been before this tragedy come back to him. Just the briefest glimmer of sense in a world where suddenly there was none. It was enough for that moment, enough to stop Varley going home and drinking himself to death or slitting his wrists because he couldn't let go of his daughter, couldn't find anything that would fill the sudden inexplicable hole in his world.

Underhill had no intention of staying but Varley had insisted. That first day he'd brought him here to this room, which had for almost three months remained untouched. Everything of Annabel's in the same place she'd left it: the clothes in the wardrobes; the stuffed animals on the bed; the Enid Blyton books on the bookshelf; the second-hand dolls' house, that Varley had saved for weeks to buy, on a table in the corner. After that first meeting Underhill had no intention of returning, but something about Varley drew him back, and something about Underhill fascinated Varley.

"All this time," Underhill said. "It was never me. It was something else that came with me. Something you needed. I didn't lift the sadness from you. Look at me – I'm not capable of that sort of thing. It was something else that made you keep wanting to invite me around. Like a drug. It lifted you away from all that shit, all that sorrow."

Varley had tears in his eyes now. "Don't be ridiculous, William. Without you here with me, I'd have never moved on. I wouldn't even *be here* today if not for you."

Underhill shook his head. "All of Annabel's things. If it wasn't for me, you'd still have something here to remember her by. You wouldn't have to keep coming in here, regretting that you packed it all up and gave it away."

"It's called moving on, Underhill. We *discussed* this. It was holding me back from getting on with my life."

"That was *me*," Underhill said. "It was… what I bring with me. What inhabits every fucking room I sit in. It watches me take a shit in the morning, it watches me lying in bed with you, it follows me into the pub, into the bank, into the hospital. *Everywhere.* All these fucking years." Underhill's voice had grown ragged. It carried into the empty room and echoed around the walls. "It made you feel that you were happier, that you were moving on, that packing up all of Annabel's things was a positive act. And so you got rid of it all and then one day you came home and you had nowhere to go to grieve save for an empty fucking room where your little girl lived. And that's on *me*." Underhill coughed and it came out like the cry of an injured animal. "That was *my* fault and we both know it. You know it, deep down, that it was because of me, because of what follows me around every moment of every fucking day."

"How can I blame you for that, William?" Varley said. He sounded lost, like Underhill had led him into a labyrinth and there was no way to know how to get out. "How can I blame you for that?"

"You can't," Underhill said. "Because you're a better man than I am. And you don't know how to let me go. And I only know one way out."

There was a moment of silence that passed between the two men. "What do you mean?" Varley said finally, his voice brittle.

"You know what I mean," Underhill said. He lifted himself to his feet quickly. He didn't want this to go any further. He didn't want to hurt this man the way he'd wanted to hurt his father. This man was decent and kind and gentle and deserved a life that Underhill didn't believe he had in him to offer. He'd only brought the toxicity of his own past to the relationship. He looked at Varley in the empty room, covered in shadows, and said, "I'm sorry. I really am. But I have to go."

Varley began to speak but Underhill turned away before he could say anything that might deter him further. Six years had been too long.

Nine

"So he's like morphine on legs," Kate said.

"Yes," Underhill said. "A big, walking, ugly-arsed anaesthetic. I'm just the bloody warm-up act in the relationship."

"You seem all right to me, William," Kate said, the wind whipping her hair into her face. She kept placing it behind her ears only it for it blow loose moments later. "Not everyone needs anaesthetising."

Kate had called Underhill before seven that morning. After last night's conversation with Varley, he couldn't remain under his roof, so he'd gone out for a walk, and once it was late enough, slunk back and slept in the motorhome, with Sorrowmouth crammed into the living area. Underhill had lain awake listening to the flea drift into a slumber, its snores vibrating the vehicle. He'd only had a couple of hours sleep when Kate had called. She sounded like she'd been awake for hours. They'd met in a cafe in town at nine but she didn't want to stay indoors. Something about surviving the fall had given her a restless quality, like a bird that had discovered it didn't need to be caged.

"How are you coping," Underhill asked. "With… what was her name?"

"Prurience."

"Prurience, right. How are you managing to stay apart like this?"

Kate shrugged. She sat cross-legged on the beach, sifting through the pebbles around her for shells. There were already a few families assembling on the beach with blankets and wind-breakers. Children having factor-50 applied to their faces and arms. The sea was rushing in just beyond their feet, and rolling away again. After a while, Kate kicked off her sandals. Her toenails were painted red. "It feels odd, I suppose. This is the longest we've been apart. It feels like having stitches tugged at. Or toothache."

It had always felt like an invisible umbilical cord to Underhill. "One time my grandad got me in the car to go for a day out in Brighton. He had a little Mini-Metro. No chance of squeezing Sorrowmouth in there. And off we went. We barely got halfway down the street before I was screaming blue-bloody-murder."

"What did you do?"

"Well, I couldn't tell him why. He just turned the car around and came home. We tried it a couple of times after that and it just kept happening. He thought I was anxious about going too far from home."

"And it's still like that?"

"It got easier once I was out of adolescence. I learned to drive without him with me. It was uncomfortable, but I could manage it for a few hours. Suffering in silence."

"How did you find out what it was Sorrowmouth wanted?"

Underhill had sketched out an abridged version of the story of his life because Kate had asked and seemed to genuinely want to know. And she was the first person he'd ever met to whom he could tell the unvarnished truth. It felt like a new chapter, like moving the story forward finally.

"It was my grandmother's funeral. Sorrowmouth was standing on the opposite side of the grave as they lowered her down. People crying. I could feel myself giving way too. And then I looked across at Sorrowmouth and I saw it. His skin started turning this dusky shade of gold. Like it was lighting up from within. And when I looked around there was this mass of colours in the air. They looked like loose black threads twisting and knotting around everyone. Sorrowmouth started moving around them, impaling them with his thorn, holding up his bowl so that this tangled mess of colours started to empty from the air into it. And everyone stopped crying for a moment. They all looked like they'd forgotten why they were there.

"Later on, at the wake, they all insisted that they'd felt my grandmother, her spirit, I suppose, lifting up from the graveside and away into the sky. They all agreed. They'd all felt it. Telling them not to be sad. They were *sure* of it."

That had been it. Underhill had seen Sorrowmouth, sitting in the corner of the function room, discombobulated and sated and he'd realised what it was, how this relationship would be defined. They'd caught each other's eye eventually and it passed between them. A tacit agreement. But then, at such a tender age, Underhill had never imagined that so little would change in the subsequent forty years. Perhaps it wasn't Sorrowmouth at all; perhaps it was just his nature. But his grandmother had insisted that he wasn't defined by his childhood. She'd said, 'You can go anywhere from nowhere,' but he'd realised long ago that if you were born in a small house, you would likely die in one too.

"Tell me about Prurience," he said, to lift him away from those memories.

"Take your shoes off first."

"Really?"

"Humour me, William. Fucking suicide risk, sitting *right* here."

"Fine." He unlaced his shoes and took off his socks, balled them inside the shoes. He got to his feet and walked to the water's edge, let the sea roll in over his bare skin.

"Satisfied?"

"Elated. How is it?" Kate asked.

"Fucking cold!" he said, but he was smiling again. It felt different, this whole thing, different to being with Varley. Unfamiliar, in a good way. He sat back down beside Kate, waiting for her to find a place to begin.

"I suppose there's this proclivity for addictive behaviour in my life. Booze, drugs, that sort of thing," she said. "But when I was fourteen there was what I'm going to call a nonconsensual sexual situation. That's all I want to say about that. I think I've given it too much air with therapists over the years, and to be honest, I don't know you well enough yet." She shrugged. "It sounds meaningless to me now. It's like this story that I've learned to tell by heart. But it's far from meaningless; I know it's still there, taking up room in my brain. It was the day after. I remember waking up and there she was, squatting in the corner of the room."

"Like him?" Underhill nodded up the beach at Sorrowmouth.

Kate glanced at him speculatively. "No, not like him, but there's a similarity I suppose. I've never even heard of this William Blake painting, to be honest. Prurience is… well, she's me, but distorted out of shape, huge and fat and spindly at the same time. Body dysmorphia, writ really fucking large. And she's always naked, so you feel like you're forever having that dream about going to work and forgetting to wear your clothes." Kate considered for a moment longer. "She looks like one of those Picasso paintings, the Cubist ones where every side of the face is two dimensional."

"And she just appeared one morning?"

It took Kate a while to realise what it was she wanted. After the shattering incident that had thrown her life out of all comprehension, her body felt like it wasn't hers anymore. She discovered that sex felt like contact, it *earthed* her. It switched off reality for a while. But the more sexual partners she had the more she realised that she was no longer at the wheel. It was Prurience, feeding on those little moments of pleasure. *La Petite Mort.* Those little deaths were what sustained her. It wasn't ever about feeling connected to someone. It had begun to feel like a transaction. A means to an end.

"Is that how it's been until now? Just you and her?"

"Yeah, up until about a year ago. I got involved with a man who seemed OK at first. He was kind and he didn't push for anything, and I felt content with him. He was happy to be with someone who didn't have to define what the relationship was. No questions about other men, other women I'd see. He did it too. Obviously he was OK with having sex a lot."

"But he changed?" Underhill said.

Kate nodded. She flexed her toes into the wet sand and closed her arms around her knees. "It got abusive.

He came back one night listing names of people he'd learned that I'd slept with. If I was a man, none of that would have mattered, would it? He wanted me to stay in his flat and not see anyone but him. When I told him that wasn't going to happen, he kept me there forcibly."

"Christ."

"It took me three weeks to get away from him. I had nowhere to go so I slept rough for a week or so. Sometimes up on the beach near where all the other homeless kip down. Sometimes I'd get into one of the shelters for a night or two, but you have to really work at it to get one of those beds. I didn't feel safe anymore. I kept seeing him in town and I'd be afraid. I hated myself for feeling like that. I started feeling like I was just repeating history, over and over. After a while I couldn't take it anymore, and well, you know the rest."

"I'm sorry, Kate," Underhill said.

They sat in silence for a while, the water washing over their toes.

"How do you feel about things now?"

"Are you asking if I intend to try killing myself again, because I botched the first attempt?"

Underhill smiled. "Maybe."

"Would you try to stop me if I tried again?"

"Would you want me to?"

"You know what, William?"

"What?"

"You've made me feel better today. Just this."

Underhill smiled, shrugged.

"And I know what you're thinking but it's not always about Sorrowmouth." She squeezed Underhill's hand. "Sometimes it's just about listening."

Ten

They texted each other over the course of the following week. They had coffee on Wednesday afternoon after Kate had been to see a therapist, and then on Thursday they met in a cafe in Hastings and went looking through the second hand bookshops and record stores. They told each other about their lives. Underhill tried to describe the visions he'd had as a child. She told him about being brought up in the wilds of Monmouthshire, before her parents split up. They were hard things to say but at the same time it was easy. The days felt lighter somehow.

Then on Friday afternoon, Kate called Underhill just as he was leaving work. She told him she had nowhere to stay. She'd been sleeping on a friend's couch and now it was unavailable, and it was too late to sit outside one of the shelters, hoping for an empty bed to become available.

"I have a motorhome," Underhill said.

"A motorhome?" Kate said, surprised. "You've been keeping that under your hat, mister. Does it work?"

"The motorhome? Yeah, I think so."

"Why don't we take it out somewhere?"

"Do you have somewhere in mind?"

She did. Underhill returned to Varley's and knocked on his door but he wasn't home. He used the key and let himself in for the first time since their conversation about Sorrowmouth, and packed a holdall with fresh clothes and toiletries. He left Varley a note, telling him he would be away for the weekend, but he'd be back and that they should discuss how to proceed. There was a clarity to his actions finally. A slow dawning of possibility which made decisions easier.

He made a silent prayer to whatever deity was listening and then turned the key in the motorhome's ignition. To his surprise it started first time. He thanked the invisible deity and reversed it out of the drive and away from Bohemia. Sorrowmouth sat cross-legged in the back, a sour look on his face. He hadn't been fed this week. He was by no means emaciated but starvation had lent him a sallow quality. He'd been feeding on scraps at the hospital and spent the evenings looking dejected. Underhill had hardly noticed. The late afternoon sun was shining. The windows were down and he felt released, better than he'd felt in years.

Underhill met Kate on the seafront. She was dressed in a long summer dress and sandals, her blonde hair gathered up on the top of her head. Her face was flushed with enthusiasm. Underhill opened the door for her and she climbed aboard with her battered old holdall. She glanced around at the interior, and at Sorrowmouth, who had squeezed himself down the hall and into the bedroom to lie on his back, staring emptily at the ceiling.

"I feel like I should have tempered your expectations somewhat," Underhill said.

Kate laughed. "Somewhat." She nodded at Sorrowmouth. "What's up with your little pal?"

"Sulking," Underhill said. "I've been starving him and he's not happy."

"Poor Sorrowmouth," Kate said, shaking her head.

"Shall we get going?" Underhill was unwilling to give Sorrowmouth any further attention. Then he spotted the odd figure skulking in the shadow of one of the seating areas on the promenade. Her naked body was twisted, her belly bloated, her hair lank and unwashed, falling into her face. It took Underhill aback for a moment. The first thing he wanted to say was: *This isn't you. This can't be how you see yourself.* But he held his tongue. Prurience stepped out of the shadows with the hesitation of someone who thinks the sun might burn them alive. She stared up at him from the kerb and he smiled encouragingly, not really knowing the etiquette. He'd become inured to Sorrowmouth and his subtle shifts in mood; he was keenly aware that Prurience would come with an entirely different set of rules, tightly woven to the delicate topography of Kate's identity.

"I woke up last night and there she was, sitting on the rug, staring at me," Kate said as Prurience finally clambered aboard. "I'd been dreaming about her every night so I knew she was on her way. I could feel her tugging on the umbilical cord."

They drove east to Dungeness. The sun was just starting to sink in the sky. The land was flatter as they passed through Rye and Camber. The only thing on the horizon was the jutting monstrous grey shape of the nuclear power station. Kate had taken out her phone and typed in the address of the Pilot Inn on Battery Road, where motorhomes and camper vans were welcomed as long as you stayed for fish and chips and a pint. Dungeness was eerily unpeopled and motionless. It didn't look like anywhere Underhill had ever seen, save for American movies set in the desert. He hadn't expected to find somewhere like this less than an hours' drive from where he'd lived all of his life.

They parked the motorhome and left Sorrowmouth and Prurience sitting at opposite ends of the vehicle, both of them silent and brooding. Underhill couldn't decide if they were aware of each other, if that was even possible. He no longer had a handle on how he felt about Sorrowmouth.

In the pub, Kate insisted on paying for the first round, and Underhill ordered the food. They sat talking in a quiet corner of the pub with monstrous portions of scampi and chips. By the time they were done, the sun had lowered below the horizon. They set out across the shingle beach, which was scattered with small wooden fishing boats. They seemed to have washed up from a different age. There were corrugated iron fisherman's huts, which only reinforced Underhill's impression of Dungeness looking like a relic of the wild west. Rusted small-gauge railway tracks stretched back to the road they'd arrived on. The tarred fisherman's dwellings all seemed to glow orange with light and rust. Kate had taken off her sandals so she could walk barefoot on the shingle. The air was thick with the honey scent of sea kale which sat like tumbleweed in the desert.

"Do you think about what life would be like without them?" Kate said.

Underhill laughed. "Only every fucking day."

"I feel like if I could just turn a corner in my mind I could see my way clear of her," Kate said. She sat down on the shingle, buried her feet in the stones. "I used to think it was just chemicals in my brain. If I could think clearly about things and get the right medication she might just vanish. *Poof,* just like that."

It had never occurred to Underhill to think that Sorrowmouth wasn't a real thing. Both of them being able to see Sorrowmouth and Prurience only muddied the waters.

"Do you touch him?" Kate asked. "*Can* you touch him?"

"I prefer not to, but he seems solid enough to me. Cold. His skin is hard and cold. And he fills rooms up with his mass. But I'm also aware that people move right through him." Underhill never saw it. There was a disconnect somewhere in his perception, as if to preserve the illusion.

"Have you stopped feeding him?" Kate asked.

"Yes." Underhill hesitated before he added: "It hasn't felt so important."

"Because of me?"

Answering that seemed like stepping into a minefield. "I've felt differently this past week," he admitted finally.

She nodded, the ghost of a smile on her lips.

"I fed Sorrowmouth because I thought it was my penance somehow. I thought that if I fed him, I would find my way back to the visions I had in my childhood. But then I realised that Sorrowmouth brought people some relief. Five minutes, an hour, a day." Underhill didn't know how that worked. Perhaps it was something to do with endorphins and serotonin. "But then I suppose it just became a habit. Like smoking or drinking. I just became Sorrowmouth's lackey. It has this boundless appetite for suffering and I ended up going looking for it. Just for a quiet life." He laughed at that. "I became a lightning rod for misery." He sat back, his hands sinking into the shingle. The stars seemed brighter out here. The sky seemed vast, endless. "But all that sorrow, all the time. It does you no good. I feel like a walking Leonard Cohen song."

At some point Kate had linked her hand with his, rested her face on his shoulder. He could feel her breath on his neck, slow and regular and steadying. "And how do you feel now?" she asked.

He squeezed her hand and kissed the top of her head. They stayed there for a while longer, listening to the sea.

Eleven

They came home on Sunday evening. Kate was going back to her friend's place to stay again. She had to be up early for a shift at the Sainsbury's near Hastings station. Underhill left her in the same place on the seafront. They kissed and she walked away. She texted him when she was back at her friend's place. He stayed in the motorhome on Varley's drive that night, unwilling to sour the weekend with what would inevitably be a difficult conversation with the man he'd shared some of his life with these past six years.

Underhill went to work the next day. He texted Kate during his lunch break and again later. He received no reply. He texted again when he got home. Still no response. He called at eight. There was no answer. He felt a peculiar sinking sensation in his gut. There was a reasonable explanation, he was sure. He was certain she'd get back to him tomorrow.

But she didn't. His calls the next day went straight to voicemail. He grew concerned for her welfare. He finished work early on a Tuesday afternoon, so he made his way into town and to the Sainsbury's. She wasn't there. He asked after her, but she hadn't come in for her shift today.

Underhill didn't know how to proceed. He couldn't decide if he'd earned the right to want to know if she was OK, but he couldn't help himself. Spending the weekend together had seemed like the first steps out of his old life and towards something new, something he couldn't yet put a name to.

He contacted a couple of the homeless shelters on Friday but they wouldn't give him any information. He didn't know her friend's number. Kate had never mentioned where it was that she lived. Underhill felt as if he'd fallen between the cracks of his old life. It had been there all this time, held in abeyance, waiting to swallow him up again. He couldn't move forward. He spent the weekend walking around the town, meandering through the neighbouring districts with an emaciated Sorrowmouth in tow, hoping that somehow, fate might conspire to bring them back together.

Another week and nothing. He stopped calling, stopped texting. Acceptance, finally. Maybe, he thought, she'd just seen sense.

Twelve

Mary texted Underhill one day a week or so later, just as he was leaving work. She wanted to know if he'd like to come over. He didn't want to go home to the motorhome, or to a vague attempt of detente with Varley. They still hadn't spoken since that evening in his daughter's room. It had felt like a full-stop on the relationship, but Underhill had not surrendered his key yet. He couldn't decide if that was what either of them wanted. He couldn't quite live with neither of them really knowing and just soldiering on through another few years before he caused some real harm. He'd sat in the motorhome, feeling stifled by the heat. He couldn't stop thinking about Kate, kept going over the events of their weekend together, reenacting the conversations they'd had, turning them over in his mind, looking for ways he might have soured things without realising. Maybe she'd just needed to tell a stranger the story of her life, someone who wasn't a therapist; someone who wouldn't try to offer her solutions to the malaise of her life. He couldn't face going back to the same routine again tonight.

Mary had been drinking all day. When she opened her front door they both stood awkwardly in the poky hallway. Sorrowmouth scratched restlessly at the empty bowl with his thorn, keenly aware that he was going to feed again finally. No more scraps from the table; an *actual meal*. Finally Mary stood on her tip-toes and hesitantly kissed Underhill. She smelled of cigarettes and spearmint chewing gum. She stepped away afterwards and said, "Let's get us both a drink," as if that was the answer to the malaise of their lives.

Underhill stood in the living room with Sorrowmouth, looking at the photos of her dead son, the crude angels in frames on the wall. He felt the vertiginous sensation of sinking into the darkness his family had made for him; there was no escaping it. You could claw your way out with learning or luck, you could scrape your way through university and set up your own business, travel the world and buy your own home, but it was always there, at the core of your being, that constant struggle to escape hardship, to aspire to something more than small houses, payday loans and zero-hours contracts. He'd thought for a brief moment that meeting Kate was a way out of that life, but he'd been mistaken.

"I've been feeling a bit off-colour these last few days," Mary said after she'd sat down with Underhill, their knees close enough to touch again. "I *miss* him," she said, a tremor in her voice. She glanced across at the shrine of photos of her dead boy, just like the one Underhill's old man had constructed in memory of his dead wife. But photos were unreliable chroniclers, Underhill felt sure. They weren't the whole story. "I dream about him, you know, coming home again and he's got dirt between his toes and under his fingernails, like he's dug his way out of the grave. Except he's *right there*." Mary pointed to the plastic urn on the top shelf of the unit beside the TV. "He was cremated."

"Did you not think of scattering his ashes somewhere?" Underhill asked.

"Like where?"

"I don't know. Did he have a favourite place? Somewhere you went on holiday?"

Mary looked perplexed. "He never went anywhere. We couldn't afford it. Butlins in Devon one year when his dad was still around. But you can't scatter someone's ashes in Butlins, can you? The holidaymakers wouldn't go much on it."

"No, I suppose they wouldn't."

"I'd rather keep them," Mary said firmly. "This is where Daniel would want to be."

Underhill nodded. Sorrowmouth was sitting in the corner, watching the dark trails of black and red and brown floating in the air above Mary's head. He pricked at the massed coils of pain until they began to drain into its bowl.

Sorrowmouth still hadn't finished by the time Mary's boyfriend arrived. He didn't knock on the door. He had his own key. Mary was falling backwards, into the soft cushions on her sofa, back into a deeper kind of reverie. Her eyes were glazing over. And then there was Arthur, Mary's on-off partner of twelve years, the man she'd never got around to mentioning, his bulk filling the doorframe. He was a man verging on late middle-age, the best of his muscles beginning to list toward fat, head shaved to a shadow across his skull, a diamond earring in his left ear. He seemed not to have realised that none of his clothes fitted him anymore. His face fell when he set eyes on Underhill with his knees touching Mary's and all the shared intimacy that implied. His eyes were too close together; his face seemed to be set in a permanent expression of befuddlement and anger. Underhill immediately moved his knees away from Mary's.

"The *fuck* is this?" Arthur demanded.

"Arthur," Mary began, her hands placatory, putting as much distance between herself and Underhill as the flat would allow. "This is William. He's a friend."

Underhill rose to reluctantly meet the man head-on.

"A friend. Right. Seems pretty fucking comfortable to me."

"We were just having a little drink."

"And what else?" Arthur asked, taking hold of Mary's jaw and staring into her eyes. "Looks like more than just booze to me."

"Don't be so fucking daft," Mary said, but Sorrowmouth continued to pierce the air now it was thick with fresh tumult. Anxiety and anger and fear. Its bowl was overflowing.

"He saved all of Daniel's things," Mary said, her voice keening now, eager to placate Arthur as quickly as possible. "The council was going to chuck everything away. He saved them all. He knew I'd want everything back."

"Look, I should be going," Underhill said and gathered up his coat. But Arthur had gone back to filling up the doorway, solid enough that Underhill had no way of pushing past without contact of some kind.

"Not so fucking fast, sunshine." Arthur placed a hand on Underhill's chest. His face was already flushed with a rising indignation. "You think you can come in here and get up to fun and games with her?"

"We didn't *do* anything!" Mary said, but she was swaying now, smiling at some indistinct pleasure, some pretty memory that had floated to the surface like fresh treasure now that all that grief had cleared from her mind.

"You're off your face, woman!"

"We just had a drink, that's all," Underhill said, his tone even.

"Fuck off!"

The force of the blow took Underhill by surprise. A fist, hard as iron, colliding with his jaw. He staggered backwards, his hand sweeping all the pictures of Daniel from the mantelpiece. The room was too small for violence. Galvanised by the success of his first blow Arthur finally stepped into the room, pushing Mary aside. She fell backwards as if in slow motion onto the sofa, her arms flung out wide. She was crying out as the photographs scattered across the floor, some of the glass cracking underfoot. Before Underhill could compose himself, Arthur had taken hold of his neck with his thick hairy hands and began to drag him from left to right in an absurd dance around the room. He elbowed Underhill in the face, once, twice, three times. Underhill slipped from Arthur's grasp and slumped to his knees. Mary was on the ground beside him, trying to gather up the photos of her son. Underhill didn't have time to raise his arms before Arthur began to rain blows down on his face, the back of his head, his neck. When he looked up finally, there was blood on the other man's knuckles, sweat stains forming around his armpits. Face flushed bright red and panting. Underhill glanced across the room. Sorrowmouth was watching it all with a dispassionate eye, pricking at the tumultuous colours in the air, filling his bowl, drinking, filling it again.

"Help me," Underhill pleaded finally, reaching out. All these years had to stand for something. Living in the shadow of the flea. He could feel the first tremors of the seizure beginning in his extremities, a stiffness jolting through his nervous system.

"No-one's going to fucking help you," Arthur said, spitting the words at Underhill's face. He hit him again and this time the world began to jolt out of true and he saw his father lurching towards him as the cola spilled across his volume of Blake's art, across 'The Ghost of a Flea'. Taking hold of him and shaking him, his teeth gritted with the sheer savagery of the act, Underhill petrified and numb, his eyes wide in terror. The memory always ended there.

Underhill came around on the street outside Mary's flat. The day had begun to pall, the streetlights were flickering to life all the way down the road. A car flew past and he heard kids jeering at him. His face felt swollen, his mouth coppery with blood. Sorrowmouth was sitting on top of a van, draining the last morsels from its bowl. Moments from the day floated up into Underhill's mind and then dispersed. Everything was out of true. His body felt stiff and brittle. He finally managed to get to his feet and stood, caught in the spotlight of the streetlamp. He glanced up at Mary's window. The light was on in the front room, but he couldn't see anyone.

He slowly began to make his way home.

Thirteen

But home still wasn't home. Underhill hesitated outside Varley's house, aching to step over the threshold and into his former lover's arms, to plead with him to nurse his wounds, tell him everything would be OK. But things weren't OK. There was no way back to Varley, no way of fooling either of them that the relationship had any more miles left to run. It was over. Underhill pressed his head to the front door for a moment, feeling a surge of emotion at the realisation that life was changing again, that there was nowhere left to go. Sorrowmouth stood at the end of the drive, staring emptily at him.

Underhill retreated to his motorhome and lay back on the bed, his mind like shattered glass. There were cuts around his head and on his arms; either from the fight or the seizure. Somehow he'd been dragged down several flights of concrete stairs too. He was amazed he'd managed to make his way home without collapsing entirely, without another seizure. Out of desperation and self-pity he'd texted Kate on the way back, but still there was no response. Finally he decided to call her but it continued to go straight to answerphone.

Underhill drifted off to sleep and dreamed of the flea, striding across the stage, through the curtains and the star-filled sky, into a shimmering world in miniature, Blake's painting like reportage from another universe. Here he found the flea lit up by footlights, a theatrical abomination beginning its performance. It paraded across its diminutive stage, minuscule and mottled with craquelure, the sky falling on its head. Somehow it had found itself summoned into being by a seance in Blake's home and sketched by the artist, and then, like a degraded facsimile, woke in Underhill's bedroom, grown out of all proportion, and hungry for human sorrow in all its abundance.

Underhill was scarcely aware that he had counted out all of the pills he had. There was more than enough to do the job. Sorrowmouth paced him from outside, moving from window to window, somehow dimly aware that Underhill was in the throes of reneging on this contract they had. They'd run out of road. This was the only way to be released from each other. He ran water into a cup.

He'd taken less than a handful when his phone lit up in the corner of his vision. He didn't want to answer it. What purpose would it serve at this point? But it stopped and then lit up again. Irritated he crossed the room and picked it up. It was Kate.

"William?" she said. He could hear the wind whipping against the phone. She was somewhere high and blustery. "I think I need you," she said vaguely. "I don't know."

"Where," he said, breathlessly. "Where are you?"

But he knew before she even told him.

Fourteen

It took Underhill a couple of attempts to start the motorhome. In between he sat breathing hard with the windows rolled down, listening to the dawn chorus all around him: a cacophony of song that might have been more pleasing in other circumstances. But then the ignition caught and the engine rattled into life. It sounded extraordinarily loud. He glanced up at Varley's window; if he'd woken him, Underhill saw no indication of it. The clarity of counting out pills seemed oddly histrionic to him now. Purity of purpose diminished those things.

When he glanced in the rearview mirror, he saw Sorrowmouth squatting in the cabin behind him, cross-legged, staring balefully into his empty bowl.

Underhill reversed the motorhome off the drive, looked one last time at Varley's house and drove away.

It took him 45 minutes to reach Eastbourne. Within the space of twenty minutes the sky turned black and he heard the first rumble of thunder, and then a dramatic fork of lightning split the sky in half. The rain came then, torrents of it, grey and unrelenting, streaming against the windscreen. Every time he had to stop for traffic lights his mind threatened him with images of Kate leaping into the air, just like his mother had all those years ago. If she'd gone back to finish the job then it was hard to imagine that she'd make the same mistake twice. But she'd *called*, hadn't she? She'd thought of him, had seen something in him that might sway her decision. He just hoped that she didn't think he wasn't coming.

By the time Underhill left the town behind and he was on the headland, he had his foot to the floor and still the rattling motorhome was only touching sixty. On either side of him, a long flat expanse of fields, all but occluded by the rain storm. He raced through the undulating lanes with the sound of the rain hammering on the roof of the motorhome until he was finally on Beachy Head Road. Underhill didn't slow down until he reached the carpark for the visitor centre. He swept the motorhome into the carpark and came to a halt. Switched off the ignition and elbowed the door open. He didn't hesitate. There were no other cars. The weather wasn't ideal for cliff walking, and it was still too early. Not yet seven a.m. Underhill didn't wait for Sorrowmouth. He dashed across the gravel as fast as his injured legs would carry him. There were no emergency vehicles in the vicinity. Surely that was a good sign? He had no idea. He crossed the road and ran across the fields, suddenly at a loss. Where to begin? Perhaps she'd already leaped and no one had been there to witness it. Perhaps someone was at this very moment attempting to coax her away from the edge. Underhill could hear his ragged breath inside his head, feel the sweat rolling in beads down his back. He was already soaked to the skin. Another fork of lightning lit up the sky. Seagulls wheeled above him, crying out. He passed signs warning him of DANGER – CLIFF EROSION and signs for SAMARITANS: THERE DAY AND NIGHT. The words seemed to call out to him, to the urges within him. A virus of language, his father had called it. There were crosses in the ground by the cliff top, small wooden shrines for suicide victims. Sorrowmouth was behind him, moving quickly without seeming to move at all. The flea wanted to linger at the shrines and scratch whatever sadness lingered there, but Underhill wouldn't stop. He was close to the edge of the cliff. The sea called out to him, the yawning expanse of air between. Vast and dark, the bruised clouds massing and shifting and rolling. There were boats in the distance, no more than specks on the horizon. Being this close to the edge made him feel curiously weightless. He still couldn't see Kate. His breath became ragged as desperation took hold. All these years he'd never felt tempted to come here, to the place where his mother had died. The place where she'd taken control of her life by taking it away from everyone else. He'd seen photographs on the internet, and the ubiquitous news reports; that was close enough. He'd thought that coming here would only compound all the queasy feelings of death that had surrounded him all his life; his notions about the cheapness of life, the option to leave everything behind if things seemed insurmountable. Coming here, being this close to the edge of the land seemed to intensify the perception that it was all too easy to simply let go. "You just keep on walking," his father had said. "There's a *certainty* to that. There's fucking *poetry* to that, boy. You make your decision and you just keep on walking. Into the air."

He ran for another ten minutes before he found her. Underhill stumbled over a steep bank and came shuddering to a halt, hands on his knees, sweat dripping from his brow, his lungs fit to burst. "Kate," he said, but the word didn't come out right and he just wheezed a long ragged breath. She wasn't at the bottom of the cliff, or at the edge of it. She was sitting on a bench a few yards away, the rain beading in her hair.

"William."

He felt his legs giving way. After the adrenaline rush there was only relief keeping him on his feet. He sat down next to Kate, breathing heavily.

"I killed her," she said.

"What?"

"I killed her. Prurience. Go and have a look."

Underhill stared at Kate for a moment more, then rose and trod carefully to the edge of the cliff. The waves were crashing and foaming across the shingle below him, and when Underhill glanced down he felt a rush of vertigo. He wanted to fall to his knees, to plant himself on the earth so that nothing would send him over the edge. Far below he could see Prurience's twisted outline, wet strands of hair covering her face. The water rolled over her and then back again. But she was entirely still.

"I talked to a policeman I met here once," Kate said. "This was a year or two ago, long before I started contemplating this. He said it was twelve seconds. That's how long it takes to hit the ground if you jump from here. I counted. It was more like ten."

"What happened, Kate?" Underhill asked. "I thought..." he fumbled with the words. His throat was closing up. "Christ. I thought you were going to be down there. I thought I was going to be too late."

"I'm sorry, William. Really, I am." She took his hand and placed it in her lap, squeezed it tightly. "But she started speaking to me."

Kate had never heard her voice before. But after the weekend she'd spent with Underhill it seemed

Prurience had a lot to get off her chest. She'd decided she didn't want Kate to be happy under any circumstances. Kate had tried to block the voice out, but it proved impossible. Prurience was there in her head before she went to sleep and she was there the moment she woke up.

"You should have called me," Underhill said. "I could have helped. I could have tried."

"I wanted to. But she wouldn't shut up. That voice, that *fucking* voice. Constant chattering in your head, constantly telling you that you're not good enough, that you're not worth shit to anyone. It grinds you down until you just agree, until you believe it's true."

Kate had bounced around the homeless shelters for several nights, and lay in poky ill-lit rooms, listening to Prurience telling her how worthless she was, that no one would want her or love her. She insisted Kate go from room to room looking for men to fuck. Finally she had no other recourse; she retreated to the one thing that had always worked, since she was fourteen. Little cuts with razorblades in the soft flesh of her arms and legs. It was enough; it quieted the voice. She could sleep.

The rain was stopping. Out over the sea, Underhill could see the sun emerging from behind the black clouds. He felt hollow. He didn't know what to say.

"I woke up this morning and I couldn't sleep, because I'd decided it was too much," Kate said. "So I borrowed some money and called a taxi and I came up here thinking that maybe I'd end it, but I'd get it right this time. Prurience was sat next to me, screaming all the way here. It felt like my head was going to split in two. I couldn't wait for it to be over. I just wanted the noise to end."

Kate looked at Underhill. "But then I thought of you. And I wanted to hear your voice one last time. So I called you. By the time I got to the edge, Prurience was in my face, literally *right in front of me*; I think she realised that she'd made a mistake. Without me there was nothing. *She* was nothing. She'd cease to exist." Prurience's voice became wheedling; gradually coaxing Kate away from the edge.

But then Kate had seen an alternative. A cold clarity had washed over her. "I just pushed her over the edge."

After a moment, Underhill said, "Is it that easy?"

Kate shrugged. "I doubt it. But it's a start, isn't it?" She smiled. "Let's call it a statement of intent."

After a moment of reflection, Underhill said: "Do you think if we put our backs into it, we can get Sorrowmouth over there too?"

Kate laughed. It was a brittle laugh but it was something. The sun emerged finally.

After a moment, she said, "He might have to come with us. For the time being."

Fifteen

It took just under a year.

Underhill gathered up his worldly possessions and Kate did the same. It didn't amount to much. They left it all on the bed in the back of the motorhome in their rush to put Hastings in the rear-view mirror. For the first couple of months they were sustained by Underhill's savings. He'd squirrelled a few thousand pounds away over the years. He'd never really wanted much. He'd always had simple needs. It kept them both afloat while they travelled, stopping in the New Forest, then Dorset and for a longer spell in Somerset. They stayed in Glastonbury near the Tor for a while and met various other travellers with stories similar to their own: the need to escape from bad families; abuse; toxic relationships. For a while Kate worked part-time at a Waitrose in Bath and Underhill picked fruit on a farm, both of them saving as much money as possible. They spent a bitterly cold winter in Salisbury. They walked around Stonehenge in the snow. Underhill started to worry that if they stayed any longer they'd turn into hippies. "It starts with macrame dreamcatchers," he warned Kate. "Then suddenly we're in tie-dye shirts and we're running around naked in the woods."

She didn't seem unduly concerned.

In spring they travelled across the Wye Valley and then north towards Snowdonia. They bought a rescue dog, a beautiful old Labrador cross who'd been found wandering, starving and alone on the A5 near Betws-y-Coed. They fed her up and took her out on the road with them, called her Birdie. They took her on long walks along empty beaches and climbed up hills, discovered a waterfall flowing through a tangle of beech trees. They stopped at pubs in tiny villages and sat in the beer gardens, eating lunch, the dog seated at their feet. One day they ran into the sea in their underwear and laughed themselves to tears as Birdie came paddling out to join them. Sometimes Underhill came back to the motorhome to find Kate with her face buried deep into the dog's fur, immersed in her smell. Her face so filled with contentment that it made his throat swell with emotion. They watched sunsets and sunrises; they lived for the delicious moment of arrival somewhere new.

Killing Prurience wasn't the end of it. Of course it wasn't; neither Kate nor Underhill thought it would be that simple to bring an end to her issues. None of it was easy, but they hadn't expected anything less. Relationships were hard work, particularly in such close quarters. They'd spent the first few months deciding if they were good enough for themselves, let alone each other. Understanding wasn't enough when all your thoughts were self-destructive. It went deeper than that. It took time but they had plenty of that. It required trust and they realised they had plenty of that too. The past was a bag of rocks that they sloughed off, one by one. This is not my stuff – from my father, the frustration and the weak will; from my mother, the fear. But these things didn't belong to them. They could be relinquished. Gradually a door opened for both of them. Underhill watched Prurience leave Kate little by little; the shadow behind her eyes diminished, day by day. Something had begun to change in him too; he felt the weight lifting from his shoulders; he saw Sorrowmouth receding to almost nothing in the rearview mirror. A paradigm shift. Daily, they were breathing fresh life into each other.

At some point, Underhill sat down and wrote letters. One to his father and one to Varley. Telling them that he was well, that he was happy, that he was sorry but he'd never go home again.

Then one day, eleven months later, Underhill woke early to the dawn chorus. It lifted him from the bed. He opened the side-door of the motor-home to let the apple-green dawn inside. The view from those open doors was a bright meadow, dappled with sunlight. There was a breeze carrying the butterflies and the bees on its uncertain tides. In the far distance was the White Horse, carved into the hillside at Westbury in Wiltshire. They had parked here a couple of days ago. They had some money saved up; they didn't need anything, just this, just each other. Birdie tumbled from the motorhome and ran into the long grass to pee.

Underhill made himself some coffee, put on his shirt and jeans. Kate was still asleep. She looked fit and tanned and healthy. They both did. He could see it, their subtle transformation in the mirror, day by day. He felt it too, every time he stepped outside on some new vista: the world was reordering itself gradually, everything was changing and lifting and becoming itself again, only more so. He went out into the meadow barefoot. Birdie came to his side and settled there. Underhill raised his face to the sun for a moment. A languid summer silence; once it had only been rented; now it felt bought and paid for. He could hear the gentle trickling of a stream nearby, the humming of bees in the lavender, the pungent scent of honeysuckle in the hedgerows. Everything was very still, everything was transformed. He felt it happen. A change. The air recomposed itself. The perfection he'd chased since childhood had been here all along, simply waiting for him to simply stop and look and listen.

Underhill opened his eyes and glanced behind him, at the motorhome, at the dog, at the open door, at the blue sky and he realised that Sorrowmouth was gone for good. He swayed for a moment in the meadows. A moment of vertigo. Then he finished his coffee and went back inside to wake up Kate.

9 781913 038748